Moscow Mules & Murder

A TIKI TROUBLE COZY MYSTERY

QUINN AVERY

ALSO BY THE AUTHOR

www.QuinnAvery.com

bit.ly/QAamazon

BEXLEY SQUIRES MYSTERIES

The Dead Girl's Stilettos

The Million Dollar Collar

The Guard's Last Watch

The Skeleton Key's Secrets

The Notebook's Hidden Truths

TIKI TROUBLE COZY MYSTERIES

Moscow Mules & Murder

STANDALONES

What They Never Said

In Her Father's Shadow

Woman Over the Edge

Looking for a steamier romance?

Check out my romantic suspense books

BOOKS BY JENNIFER ANN

www.authorJenniferAnn.com

Now on Kindle Unlimited

KENDALL FAMILY SERIES

Brooklyn Rockstar

Midwest Fighter

Manhattan Millionaire

Oceanside Marine

Kendall Christmas

Miami Bodyguard

American Farmer

ROCK BOTTOM SERIES

Outrageous

Notorious

Courageous

Ferocious

STANDALONES

Broken Little Melodies

The Secrets Between Us

FALLEN HEROES DUET

Saving Phoebe

Saving Alexa

MC ROMANCE SERIALS

Inferno Glory MC

Jawa's Angels MC

NYC LOVE SERIES

Adam's List

Kelly's Quest

Chloe's Dream

This is a work of fiction. Names, characters, business, events and incidents are the products of the author's imagination. Any resemblance to actual persons, living or dead, or actual events is purely coincidental.

No part of this book may be reproduced in any form or by any electronic or mechanical means, including information storage and retrieval systems, without written permission from the author, except for the use of brief quotations in a book review.

Any trademarks, service marks, product names or named features are assumed to be the property of their respective owners, and are used only for reference. Namely: Ford Bronco, Vespa, "Yummy" lyrics by Justin Bieber, Adidas, *Stranger Things*, Lord Farquaad, Shrek, *Law & Order*, Olivia Benson, David Bowie, Soundgarden's *Superunknown*, Barbie, *Sweet Caroline*, Nancy Drew, AC/DC, Chandler and Monica (of *Friends*), Joker and Harley Quinn (of *Batman*), Stormbringer (my favorite band!), Nirvana's *In Utero*, Speedos, Chippendales

The important thing is to not stop questioning. Curiosity has its own reason for existing.

-Albert Einstein

ONE

Until the night I found a human skull, my life had been relatively static. As I balanced on my tip-toes, tongue lodged between my teeth, sweat trickling down my aching back, right arm extended far over my head in an attempt to hang a sign advertising the tiki bar's next drink special, I convinced myself there were worse things than living said static existence.

"High enough?"

"Your sense for decorating is worse than my ninety-year-old grandfather's, and he has glaucoma in both eyes." Beckett sounded like he was right behind me.

I glared over my shoulder. "Then why don't you

hang this? You do remember I'm your shortest friend, right?"

He rolled his emerald green eyes before pressing his fists against his hips in a superhero pose. "The special doesn't start until tomorrow night anyway. If you can't get it, I'll have Molly help me in the morning."

With a determined grunt, I bent my knees and jumped for the roof of the tiki bar. My stomach jutted in the other direction when my toes lost contact with the edge of the stool, and I became airborne. I landed face down with my hands trapped beneath me. Santa Maria Island's white quartz sand may have been the softest in the state, but it did little to cushion my fall. To add insult to injury, the vinyl sign I was attempting to hang floated down over my head.

Beckett burst out laughing. "Zo! Are you okay?"

I wiggled an arm out from beneath me to flash a thumbs up. "Never been better."

He scooped me out of the sand and assisted me back onto my bare feet. "I'll never understand how you can rip up a dance floor, but everywhere else you have the coordination of a newly-born baby giraffe."

Brow furrowed, I shook the sand from my long red hair and excessively freckled skin. Thanks to my mom's Irish heritage, I was often mistaken for a teenager despite being on the cusp of twenty-five.

Beckett grabbed my arm and batted his long lashes. He teetered on the hotter side of movie star handsome, and he knew it. "Any chance I can sweet talk you into closing up for me? I have somewhere to be."

"You always have somewhere to be," I muttered, admittedly a little jealous. My social calendar was as empty as a bottle of house tequila after margarita night. "Maybe *I* have plans."

"Binge watching *Stranger Things* for the umpteenth time *doesn't* qualify as 'plans', Zo. Pretty please?" he begged, sticking out his bottom lip. "I'll bring Dee Dee's tomorrow."

The offer perked my interest. Dee Dee's Donuts were my biggest weakness. Still, he had done a far better job of bribery in the past. "And?"

He puffed out his cheeks, thrusting a hand into his perfectly styled dark flow. "And I'll do your dishes at the end of your shift."

"And?"

"Seriously, Zo. You want a vial of my blood, too?"

I slammed the palm of my hand into his beauti-fully sculpted collarbone. "Last time I closed for you, you took me up to Clearwater for a night of *dancing*.

Do you know how long it's been since someone took me dancing?" From the moment I could walk, I had taken dance classes all the way through my senior year in high school, then I'd continued with a hip-hop club in college. "I'm getting tired of having to dance alone in my bedroom with earbuds. If my landlady hears me play anything other than Elvis, she bangs on my door and claims her ears are bleeding."

"This is exactly why you need a boyfriend. Living with an insane old widow is detrimental to your health."

"Teenie is not *insane*. She's a saint to let me and Molly live with her."

"You're missing the point. At this stage in your life, you should be shacking up with some hottie who worships your every move." He grabbed my other arm and shook me. "Look at you, Zoey Zastrow! You're adorable, and funny, and sweet, and one of the nicest humans to inhabit this planet! It's a travesty that you're still single—a disservice to twenty and thirty-something year-old stud muffins in all of Florida! It's time you realize not all men are two-timing jerks, and go forth into the dating pool."

"Have you *seen* the dating pool for my age bracket?" I huffed, twisting out from his grip. "That water is tainted. It's full of mommas' boys who spend their days gaming in their parents' basements. I may as well date a hobbit."

"That might not be so bad. At least hobbits appreciate the value of food." Shrugging, he dug the keys to his Vespa out from his pocket and wiggled them in the air. "I promise I'll take you dancing if you'll promise you'll give the dating thing a try."

Before I could open my mouth, he smothered me in a designer-cologne-scented embrace. "Thanks, Zo! You're the best!"

He left quickly, probably because he didn't want to hear me say no. That's the trouble with good friends. They do things regardless of what you want.

I gazed past Beach Bummers' dark tiki bar to the moon-lit water beyond, reminding myself I was in paradise. After over two years of calling the island home, the briny smell and rushing sound of the Gulf's waves crashing onto the beach still gave me a sense of peace.

Fleeing South to waitress hadn't been anywhere on the vision board I'd created for my goals after college. My meticulously thought-out plan involved two years of post-grad in something-or-other that would earn me a fat stack of cash, then I would marry my long-term boyfriend before we moved to Duluth where Todd would become a successful trial lawyer, and I would stay home to raise our three beautiful children in a newly constructed waterfront home.

Then, mere moments before our commencement ceremony, the man who after that moment would forever be known as "Todd the Terrible" announced he was crushing my dreams for a big-bosomed State cheerleader.

That night, during a meltdown that involved the champagne intended for our celebration (purchased with the assumption that Todd the Terrible was going to propose), I made the decision to pack my worldly possessions and drive south the next morning until it no longer felt like my world was ending. I guess my situation didn't seem quite as dire once I reached the stunning white-quartz beaches on Santa Maria Island several days later.

Although waitressing at Beach Bummers was only supposed to be temporary until I found a job that utilized my bachelor's degree in business, I quickly became fond of my boss, the staff, the patrons, the beachfront location, and the generous tips.

With a resolved hum, I turned away from the water and popped my earbuds in, dancing to

Justin Bieber while checking off the list of chores to be completed. By the time I had wiped down the tables and bar top, cleaned the bathrooms, straightened the stools and chairs, turned off every neon sign and rope light, mopped and locked the tiki bar, then gathered all the garbage, I was spent. And the most daunting task was yet to come.

The 10 yard dumpster was located on a patch of grass behind the 3-story resort, next to the employee parking lot. The contents stunk to high heaven from the brutal strength of the sun, and there were often nefarious critters lurking inside. I mentally crossed my fingers when flipping the lid open, praying a stray feline with a perilous meow would be the worst of my discoveries.

"You better take me dancing somewhere awesome, Beckett Barnett," I muttered, lugging the first trash bag over my shoulder. I heaved them in one at a time. The final bag was full of empty liquor bottles and required the use of both hands. The weight of it jarred me sideways. Both me and the contents of the bag spilled out across the narrow patch of grass. The top of my head collided with the dumpster.

Would anyone notice if I started wearing a helmet to

work? I mused, scrambling back to my feet and rubbing my sore head.

Over the next ten minutes, I gathered the contents of the bag and pitched handfuls of bottles into the dumpster. On a normal night, I would worry about waking guests. But it was late, I was tired, and the stench made my gut churn. By the time I located what I thought was the last bottle, it took a moment for my brain to register the object pinned beneath my fingers. It was white, round, and smooth with two dark sockets.

And it was smiling at me.

A noiseless scream ripped from my lips as my heart gave a thunderous roar.

It was a human skull.

There was a dead human being. In my employer's parking lot.

As the Biebs was cooing, "you got that yummy, yum," in my ear.

The skull was partially buried, surrounded by small piles of dirt. One of the nefarious creatures that I feared I would cross had probably scratched the ground to unearth it, and said creature had given up when the large prize refused to give way.

Maybe it was only a prop. Smith, my boss, was known for throwing elaborate pirate parties. I bent on rubbery legs and rapped on the top of the skull with my knuckles.

Knock knock.

Who's there? I imagined it asking.

The dense bone smarted against my knuckles.

It was definitely real.

My breaths became tiny, panic-ridden bursts. I yanked my earbuds out and peered over my shoulder, wishing someone—*anyone*—was around. I'd even settle for the usual gaggle of drunk guests cackling like school girls and slurring songs from their glory days.

It obviously wasn't an emergency worthy of 9-1-1 even if it sort of felt like one. But what if I didn't call the police, and they found my fingerprints on the skull? Would I be considered a suspect? Would they think I had buried the person, then came back to visit their remains like a sentimental psychopath?

Despite the twist in my gut, I forced myself to study it closer. It was smallish, but not quite the size of a child's. More than likely, it belonged to a woman. Something inside its mouth caught in the moonlight, sparkling.

Was the rest of the person's body buried beneath? Did it mean the poor soul wasn't given a proper burial? How had they ended up here?

Underneath the jaw, a white plastic card lay partially exposed. It looked an awful lot like the security cards every Beach Bummers employee carried. Reaching for it with one hand, I covered my face with the other, wincing while peering through my fingers. After I plucked the card out from the dirt, the skull laughed at me.

It *laughed*.

What a chicken! it seemed to be saying. *Did you think I was going to bite?*

Then I realized the jaw had only moved because something was inside its mouth. A blue crab scurried out sideways, snapping its demon claws at me. Although I had learned to tolerate many of Florida's creatures since moving to the warm state, crabs were not among that list.

With the card still clutched in my fist, I fell back on my other hand, ironically crawling away from the crab *like* a crab.

Once I was able to get my limbs to cooperate, I ran the entire way home.

TWO

My first waking thought was of the laughing skull.

Guilt for leaving it behind weighed heavy on my shoulders. What if something had returned in the night to take it away? Remembering the creepy crab, I shuddered. While I doubted it could've carried the skull away, I had witnessed stranger phenomenons since my move to Florida. I once watched a 10-foot alligator stroll down the beach with a pool noodle clutched in its jaw, and gators aren't even indigenous to the area.

Yawning, I plucked my phone off my night stand to check the time. Molly had sent a string of texts at 4 a.m.

Staying with a 👤 2nite

Remember the one in that group from 🏴 the other night?

Their rental is 🌑 in a good way.

Tell Teenie I'm 👌

I blew out a heavy breath. An abundance of emojis always meant she had gone well beyond her tolerance. I hated thinking about my best friend going home with attractive strangers only on the island for a short visit. Just because she was two years older didn't mean she was any wiser.

At least Teenie would be gone for water aerobics, and not around to project her frustrations with Molly onto me. Teenie was an avid fan of true crime shows, and regularly informed us of all the manipulative ways attractive serial killers were able to get by with murder for decades. It was Teenie's greatest fear that she would turn on the news one morning to discover Molly had been Ted Bundy-ed.

Tossing my fluffy duvet aside, my eyes swept over the contents of my spacious bedroom. Molly and I had been fortunate when Teenie, the zany senior citizen who frequented Beach Bummers, offered us each our own room in the 10-year-old bungalow at a ridiculously low rate. After her husband of over fifty years had died from a heart attack just months after they'd built their dream home, she was desperate for companionship. As my rental at the time was destroying two-thirds of my paychecks, I jumped with the generous offer.

Beckett had been sorely wrong about my eye for decorating. The soft palate of colors I'd chosen to accentuate the white walls produced a cozy coastal vibe. Colorful shells filled a lantern atop an antique vanity that had once belonged to my great, great grandma. My mom had helped me refurbish it with robin's egg blue chalk paint, and I gave the same treatment to a nightstand I found on the side of the road. I'd purchased a $20 cabinet from a thrift store to hold my flatscreen TV. Beneath it was a shelf of unique picture frames with photographs of me with Teenie and the Beach Bummers crew, and my mom's last visit. My most recent purchases included a stunning illustration of the island at sunset painted by a regular bar patron.

When I realized the painting hung crooked, I attempted to adjust it with a frown. Maybe Beckett *hadn't* been so wrong.

Clearing the sleep from my eyes, I stumbled into my attached bathroom and peered into the half-wall mirror over my vanity. My elbow-length, fiery red hair was still damp from the shower I'd taken before crashing in the night. The freckles spilling from the bridge of my nose onto my cheeks shone bright without foundation. Sometimes people told me I was pretty. Most of the time, like with Beckett, I was almost always described as either cute or adorable. No one had ever called me beautiful (especially not Todd the Terrible), although I supposed that was a term reserved for goddesses with Molly's flawless features. "Pretty" seemed fair enough.

Noting the way my chestnut eyes—so dark that I've been asked why I don't have irises—were shadowed from working late, I once again thought of the poor skull in the parking lot. The rest of the body must've been buried underneath. The person deserved a proper burial in a cemetery, or a place on a mantle. Surely someone missed them. Their loved ones needed to know they had passed.

With that thought, I decided it was my duty to report my discovery to the police. I secured my hair into a high ponytail before changing into gray running shorts, a lightweight tank top in a bold turquoise, and my favorite pair of sneakers. The station was just over a mile and a half away, and a good run would clear thoughts of the laughing skull from my head.

It was a beautifully cloudless Friday morning, and the charming island was alive with locals. I ran through my neighborhood of properties inland, mainly condos and lower-income housing intended for the island's service industry workers and travelers on a budget. Then I veered toward prime waterfront lots where a few 5-star restaurants nestled among elegant villas painted in Caribbean pastels, towering three or four stories high with balconies on every level that provided a proper jaw-dropping view of the turquoise Gulf. Some were built specifically as rentals with only a third or so occupied year-round by corporate types wealthy enough to retire long before they were riddled with arthritis and body parts in need of replacing.

The city was thirty blocks long and ten wide. Its zoning laws required businesses downtown to use limited choices of paint colors and fonts on their storefront. It resulted in a quaint, uniformed appearance that drew tourists like ants to a gooey popsicle stick. Deep porches with white columns provided outdoor seating for those businesses that shared the 2-story buildings. The store owners typically lived in the studio apartments above, while the first level targeted visitors in the form of ice cream parlors and souvenir shops, rental agencies for homes and motorized rentals. Locals frequented most of the restaurants, especially Polly's Pizza and Dee Dee's Donuts.

On Main Street, a handful of tourists buzzed about on 6-person golf carts, retro bicycles, and neon-colored mopeds. I waved at every shop owner opening for the day, and called out to the usual locals waiting on the sidewalk. I knew nearly every permanent resident of the island by sight, if not by name, and they all knew the redheaded waitress from Beach Bummers.

As I passed the pink and white striped awning over Dee Dee's, I began to salivate in a Pavlovian response. I suspected Dee Dee snuck crack into her recipes. Just as with any other day during tourist season, an abundance of customers queued around the block. I could skip the line by waving at Dee Dee, then meeting her for my usual Bavarian cream with pink frosting and white sprinkles in the back alley like some kind of drug deal (more proof supporting my theory that she used crack). I resisted, however, reminding myself that Beckett had promised to bring donuts later.

The police station was a small, white stucco building in the dead center of town. Its location marked the beginning of the end of the touristy hot spots, giving way to essential trades like dental offices and law firms, auto repair shops and clinics for both people and pets. Its sea green hurricane shutters had recently been repainted, and a crisp American flag proudly waved high above the clay roof with the State of Florida flag underneath. I tugged on the glass door etched with the official department's name, finding it locked.

Blowing out a red curl that had escaped from my hair band, I plopped down on the stone steps and ran my bubble gum pink fingernails over my teeth. *Should I have brought the skull along, or would that have been considered interfering with a crime scene?* Then I belatedly remembered the employee card in my pocket. *Too late to worry about interfering. How would I even go about starting the conversation?*

"Oh hey, I found a laughing skull," I muttered in a wheezy breath.

I was startled by a deep chuckle. "What was that?"

I knew everyone who worked with the local police department. Chief Shaw and his wife were regulars at Beach Bummers, and Avery, the station's office administrator, lived two blocks down the street from Teenie's house. The only deputy had relentlessly hounded me for a date after I first moved to the island.

I had never laid eyes on the tall, dark, and dreamy man with an athletic build crawling out of a classic off-road vehicle parked at the curb. Between his sky-blue button-down featuring a white palm leaves print, khaki shorts, and tan sandals, I wouldn't have guessed that he was a man of the law if it hadn't been for the gold badge pinned to his shirt.

My throat dried when I took in his dark brown flow with a shaved part on one side, and thick eyebrows nestled over eyes the color of melted chocolate. Despite the hard, masculine angles of his bronzed nose and square jaw, he had a kind face and lips that appeared as heavenly soft as a down pillow. When he threw me a little wave, I noted a wildlife tattoo covering his forearm that disappeared beneath the short sleeve.

"*You got that yummy, yum,*" the Biebs sang in my head.

"I...uh...want to report a murder," I blurted. "At least I think. I found a skull. An old one. It didn't have any flesh on it or anything. It was smallish, but bigger than a child's. More like the size of mine. I'm ninety-nine percent certain it was real, but I'm no archaeologist. I'm just a waitress. At Beach Bummers tiki bar. Maybe you've heard of it? On the beach?" I wanted to slap myself. *Since when was I a rambler?* "That's where I found it—the skull."

One of his dark eyebrows playfully quirked. "You've come to the right place. I'm the new detective on the island." My bones liquefied onto the steps when he threw me an adorable smile over perfectly straight white teeth. It was a mouth made for a toothpaste commercial.

He offered his large, notably tanned hand. "Grayson Rivers."

Electricity zapped my palm when I buried my hand inside his. His skin was soft, and there was a lot of strength behind his grip. "Zoey Zastrow."

He drew me up to my feet with very little effort, bringing me within inches of his handsome face. The scent of his sandalwood cologne made my belly all fuzzy and tingly.

"Let's go inside, Zoey," he suggested, releasing my hand. The deep roll of his voice tinged with a slight West Coast accent only added more fuzzies. "This humidity is killing me."

In a daze of exploding hormones, I nodded and waited behind him as he fiddled with the lock. Going to the police station that morning had been the best idea *ever*.

When the detective pushed his way inside, he closed his eyes with the blast of AC and tipped his head back. "That's better."

The urge to lick his protruding Adam's apple like a lollipop niggled my tongue. "It's not even noon yet, Detective," I reminded him with a soft giggle. "How long have you been on the island?"

With a sheepish grin, he shrugged. "I just moved here from California last week. I guess it'll take a while to adjust."

Based on his usage of pronouns, I hoped it meant he had made the trip alone and hadn't brought a wife and kids. I felt a twitch of shame when I realized I might be fantasizing about getting down and dirty with someone else's man.

With another heart-failure-inducing smile, he motioned me past the receptionist's desk. "Come on back, Zoey."

Every time he uttered my name in that sexy voice of his, I was sure my heart would catapult out from my chest and land inside his hands.

He led me into the office adjacent to the chief's. It barely accommodated a bookcase, two sets of filing cabinets, and a desk. Small cardboard boxes occupied the metal chairs intended for guests, and the walls were stark white. A set of double hung windows provided a perfect view of the customers gathered outside Dee Dee's Donuts. My stomach gurgled with jealousy.

"Sorry about the mess," Grayson told me. "I haven't had time to settle in, and our administrator has been out sick."

"It's...*cozy*." Calling it "bland" would've seemed rude. "Could use a touch of color and some pictures on the walls." I studied the illustrations on his arm. The detailed wolf howling at the moon suited his alpha persona. "Maybe something with wildlife."

He released a deep, delicious chuckle. "Maybe I should hire you to fix it up for me." As he removed a box from one of the chairs, I noted his left ring finger was delightfully bare. "Have a seat, Zoey. I want to hear more about this skull." His arm brushed against mine when he bent to set the box on the floor.

With my heart dancing to a frantic tango, I lowered to the chair and watched him lower behind the desk. The way his broad shoulders shifted as he reached for a notebook and pen made my toes tingle. It had been forever since I had felt undeniably attracted to anyone. So long that I nearly forgot it wasn't socially appropriate to sigh out loud in appreciation.

"Last night I was closing for Beckett, my friend-slash-coworker," I explained, quickly averting my eyes away from his tattoo. It probably wasn't appropriate to ogle his body like a psycho either. "He's always asking me to cover for him even though he knows I despise closing, but it's whatever."

"You said this is at Beach Bummers?" he asked, scribbling in the notebook.

"That's right. It's on the north end of the island. Our tiki bar is the best hangout around—always busy. You should come there for dinner and drinks some night. Smith, my boss, is amazing, and everyone who works there is crazy friendly. Did I mention it's right on the beach?" My throat tightened as I imagined him only wearing a pair of swim trunks. That was something I needed to see as soon as humanly possible. "You could come *tonight*—I waitress from four to close."

Instead of calling me out for being a crazy rambler, he grinned. "I might have to do that."

My cheeks warmed, which was never good with my complexion. In a few more seconds, I would become as red as a clown's nose. "Anyway, I was throwing garbage into the dumpster behind the building, and I...er...dropped one of the heavy bags. I bent to pick everything up, and that's when I found it, half exposed in the dirt. It looked like an animal had dug it up. I thought at first..." More heat rushed through my cheeks when I remembered how he had chuckled when I had inadvertently mentioned the laughing skull. "You know what? Never mind."

He tilted his head to the side. "You thought what?"

"It's nothing. I uh...just saw the jaw...move. Turns out one of those terrifying blue crabs was camping out inside. I'm not too fond of crustaceans, so I...uh...ran. Home."

If he deemed my reaction to be ridiculous, I couldn't tell by his friendly expression as he nodded with understanding. "What time was this?"

"A little after three?"

His thick brows drew down like angry caterpillars. "You were closing the bar alone at three in the morning?"

"It's no big deal, Detective. Our worst crimes involve visitors skipping out on their dinner bills." When his frown didn't lift, I tried using a lighter tone. "Besides, I'm not *alone*, alone. There's always someone running the front desk inside the resort, and it's always booked solid with dozens of guests. Some of them are pretty wasted by that time of night, but they're harmless. They usually just want to sing something ridiculous like *Sweet Caroline*...and they sometimes want to dance. Who doesn't like to dance?"

"Those guests you speak of might not always be so harmless," he grunted in a deeper tone. "You should at least carry pepper spray. And please, call me Grayson."

All at once remembering the card, I dug into the hidden pocket in my shorts. "I found this underneath the...uh...skull. Its jaw. I know I probably shouldn't have touched it, but I had to see if it was what I thought it was. Then that horrible crab charged at me, and I didn't realize I was still holding onto it until I got home." I held it out to him.

He carefully gripped the card's edges to examine it closer. "What is it?"

"It's a security card from Beach Bummers. At least I think. This one looks old and the bar logo is a little different. Every employee is given one. They track our activity, from unlocking the register to checking in and out of our shifts."

"Interesting." He dug through one of his desk's drawers and produced a clear baggie, then dropped the card inside. "Do you have time to take me to this skull and show me the exact spot you found this?"

It was difficult to resist shuddering when I thought of the crab. "Yeah, but the tiki bar is at the other end of the island, and I sold my car after I moved here. Seemed like a silly expense when I could run or take the Gorilla Bus anywhere."

"Gorilla Bus?"

"It's a free shuttle service, driven by volunteers that work for tips. Some of them drive like maniacs, and some stink like—" I bit my tongue, deciding if I said *weed*, I would be ratting the drivers out to law enforcement, "—ummm, sweaty man, but it's a cheap way to get around."

With a chuckle, he stood. "I'll drive as long as you don't mind running next door with me first. I've been dying to try those donuts." He threw me the most charming wink in the history of hot guy winks. "My treat."

There was no muting the appreciative sigh that fell from my lips.

THREE

Grayson pulled his parrot orange Bronco alongside Beckett's baby blue Vespa in the Beach Bummers parking lot. I ran my fingers along the Bronco's black dashboard before I hopped out from the passenger's door. I could've continued riding around in his open-air vehicle for hours. Every last accessory appeared to be as old as the truck, and the white vinyl bench was free of stains or tears. Either Grayson was a bit of a neat freak, or he had restored the truck to its original beauty. Although there hadn't been much conversation as we devoured our donuts, both the vehicle *and* its owner were a pleasant sight to behold.

"What a cool little truck," I declared to Grayson. "I love going topless."

A choking laugh burst from his lips. "What?"

"I meant in your Bronco!" I exclaimed, shaking my ponytail. "You know, with the top off! The truck's top, not mine!" I momentarily webbed my hand over my burning face. "Seriously. Can we please pretend I didn't just say that?"

"In that case, I enjoy going topless, too." His deep voice rumbled with another laugh. "And you're right, the truck is cool. It was given to me by my grandpa. He bought it new for my grandma in sixty-nine, but she hardly ever drove it anywhere because she couldn't get a hang of the three-speed manual transmission. I had it transported here on a flatbed trailer so I wouldn't rack up extra miles."

"Knowing it has always been in your family makes it even cooler," I decided, grinning up at him. As we neared the dumpster, I pointed off to the side. "That's where I found it." I cringed at the dramatic tone my voice took when I added, "*The skull.*"

"Let's go check it out."

As we walked side-by-side, I was hyper aware of our height difference. At 5'3", almost everyone towered over me. Grayson must've been over six feet tall. Todd the Terrible had only been 5'7" and possessed a massive Lord Farquaad complex. Much like the *Shrek* character, he would pitch a fit if anyone dared to make him feel small—especially if I ever wore high heels.

"I don't see it," Grayson announced, turning to face me.

"See what?" *The skull,* I quietly chided myself. "Oh yeah. Uh...over here." I squared up in front of the green dumpster, envisioning the trajectory of the trash bag, and moved off to the side. It was nowhere in sight. "Where is it?" I muttered, spinning around.

I nudged the toe of my sneaker at the lump of dirt where I was sure the bag had landed. "I'm not crazy," I insisted. "I mean, I was tired, but not '*I see dead people*' level of tired. Something creepy-crawly must've carried it away in the night. You have no idea how many nefarious creatures live down here." Feeling the burn of embarrassment crawling up my nape, I twisted back around to Grayson. "It was *right here*. I'd swear my life on it."

He flashed the palms of his hands. "Don't worry. I believe you."

"But you can't launch an investigation without it, right? I mean...what if the rest of the body isn't buried here?" I gnawed on my bottom lip. "What if the killer did away with it some other way, and only kept the head? Maybe they came back to visit their trophy, and decided to take it home so they didn't have to keep coming back here." I covered my face with my hands. "You must think I'm crazy. Even *I* think I sound crazy."

"That's not at all what I'm thinking." When I removed my hands from my face, he dangled the bagged employee card between us. "I'm actually thinking we should have a conversation with your boss. Then I'll decide if the situation merits a full investigation."

A smile crept over my lips. "I'll take you to meet him."

He followed closely behind me around the side of the resort to the stone path through the powdery sand that led to the tiki bar. Although it didn't officially open until 11, a few regulars lounged on the rainbow selection of stools beneath the thatch roof and colorful lights swaying to the steel drum music. Some played a game of cards, some drank coffee and gossiped about the locals. As long as alcoholic drinks weren't ordered at that hour, Smith never turned anyone away.

From where Molly wiped down a table, she spotted me and immediately sashayed in our direction with a spark in her captivating blue eyes. She tugged on the knot tied at the bottom of her uniform, causing the swells of her double Ds to pop out from the shirt like a tube of crescent rolls. Beneath extra short black cotton shorts, her deeply tanned legs stretched on for miles.

There was no denying Molly McGregor was a vixen—the kind who could've pulled off an actual set of horns and a tail. She was runner-up for Miss Southern Florida before meeting me, and had won every wet t-shirt contest she entered.

My shoulders sagged. It would only take one flash of my bestie's insidious smile to place Grayson under her spell. As soon as I realized the mere idea of Molly hooking up with the detective made me green with envy, I swallowed back a snort. Who was I to say he would be interested in me anyway? I had acted like a squirrel on caffeine in his office, then made the ridiculous comment about riding topless.

"Well hello there," Molly greeted us, flipping her smooth black hair over one shoulder. Her tongue slipped over her ultra white teeth and her gaze darkened. "Who's your handsome friend, Zo?"

"Detective Grayson Rivers," he told her in a formal voice, thrusting his hand her way.

Molly's meticulously arched eyebrows lifted as

she gingerly shook his hand like a weirdo. "A *detective*?" Her oversized false lashes fluttered and she held her fingertips over her lips. "Are you here to *arrest* me?"

"Tone it down, *Lohan*," I said, nudging my hip against hers. "He said he's a detective, not a B-movie director."

Grayson coughed into his hand, muting a chuckle. "I'm here on official business."

"Oh crap!" Molly gasped, eyeing his badge. "Does Zoey need a lawyer? I guess it really is like Teenie always says—the ones you least expect sometimes just snap. I'm lucky she didn't decide to stab me in my sleep." With a hand on her cocked hip, she turned to me. "What'd you do, Zo?"

"None of the psychotic things you're suggesting, but thanks for the vote of confidence." I glanced around the bar. "Is Smith around?"

Molly stage-whispered, "He's 'taking inventory'."

The term was Smith's not-so-secret code for "nap time." The former rock and roll frontman hated to admit that he was old enough for a snowbird discount. He would rather brag how he had toured dozens of countries in the 80s, sometimes staying awake for days in a row to party. Since turning sixty, he required a short nap by noon and was often in bed by ten.

"I'll bring him out," I offered. Without thinking, I wrapped my fingers around Grayson's forearm. The one with the engaging tattoo. "I'll be right back." Before I headed inside, I shot Molly a stern look, warning her to behave.

She flashed an innocent smile. "Don't worry. I'll keep him entertained."

That's what I'm afraid of, I huffed to myself. I was a handful of yards from the building when Beckett darted in alongside me. "Who's Mister Tall, Dark, and Hella Handsome?"

"His name is Grayson Rivers, and he drives the coolest truck you've ever seen." A coy smile curled my lips. "He's the new police detective on the island."

Beckett hummed in a skeptical noise. "Since when does the island need a detective?"

"I have no idea, but you won't hear any complaints from me."

He let out a loud gasp. "Does this mean you're finally going to break your dry spell?"

"It means I have no clue how to act around him." Inside the resort's lobby, I stopped to fist the front of my friend's work shirt. "The guy is crazy gorgeous, and lightyears out of my league, Beck! You would've been so disappointed the way I spazzed out when I first met him. I've never rambled on like that before. You'd think someone had fed me a handful of quarters."

"Breathe, Zo." He pried my hands off his blue button-down and gave me a condescending pat. "I'm sure it wasn't as bad as you're imagining. What's he doing here?"

"Last night, while I was doing *your* job for you, I found a skull out back."

His emerald eyes bulged. "Like a *human* skull?"

"No, a parrot skull," I retorted. "He's here to investigate whether or not Polly choked on a cracker."

Beckett clicked his tongue. "Someone had a bowl of snark for breakfast."

I was ready to correct him by saying I'd in fact had the Dee Dee's he had promised me when Smith materialized behind us.

"What's this snark?" his gruff voice interjected. "That some kind of new drug you kids are doing nowadays?"

Even though Smith hid behind his favorite pair of mirrored aviator glasses, it was evident the Ohio native had lived a hard life. Graying stubble around his dimpled chin, deep creases untanned in his leather-like skin, vintage Pink Floyd t-shirt worn thin, and a crackled voice from years of screaming into a microphone were only the beginning traits of an ancient rocker who'd seen and done it all. Though he'd given up the lifestyle of groupies and drugs, I was convinced "party like a rockstar" was a term coined from his adventures. I fondly regarded him as my zany surrogate grandfather.

I hooked my hand beneath his armpit, and steered him out of the lobby. "I need you outside."

He palmed his short brown hair with hesitation as he often did, as if expecting it to be shoulder-length as it was in his younger days. "What—"

"Zoey found a skull on the property last night," Beckett blurted, rushing back in beside us. "She brought her future husband to investigate."

I elbowed him in the ribcage. "Stop."

"Always something with you two." Smith grunted in a half humored, half irritated sound. "You're talking about what...a *human* skull?"

"Yes, human," I confirmed with a huff.

"It's a little early for that kind of thing," Smith said. He pulled a cigarette from his back pocket.

Although he had given up smoking over a decade prior, he often held one between his lips, unlit. I'd long since decided it was either to complete his image, or because it gave him comfort. "I'm gonna need one of your blueberry mules, Beckett. Heavy on the vodka."

Beckett promptly veered toward the bar. "Consider it made."

I continued to guide Smith to where Grayson occupied one of the larger tables in Molly's section. My traitorous best friend leaned over him with her elbows on the table, giggling excessively. Grayson was making an obvious attempt to avert his gaze anywhere other than the twinned melons thrust into his face.

Maybe stabbing my roommate in her sleep wasn't too far outside of the realm of possibility, I thought bitterly.

Grayson caught his reflection in Smith's sunglasses and stood. "Detective Grayson Rivers, sir. Thank you for taking the time to meet with me."

Smith took his time sizing the detective up and down before shaking his hand with one pump. "Smith Dillon."

"Smith bought this property twenty years ago and turned it into the most popular and successful destination spot on the Gulf side," I informed Grayson. I couldn't explain why I was so eager for the two men to hit it off, but the need gnawed at me like a hungry beaver. I turned to my boss. "Detective Rivers recently moved here from California."

"California, huh?" Smith sniggered. "I'll give it two weeks tops before you're ready to move back. This island couldn't be any more different from Hollywood, son."

"That's exactly why I transferred here," Grayson replied, lowering to his chair. "Go ahead and have a seat, Mr. Dillon. I have a few questions pertaining to the skull found by your employee."

"What?" Molly yelped, slapping a hand over her chest. "Like, a real one?"

"What's with you people?" I challenged. One would think I had included the fact that I originally thought it had been laughing. "Yes, a real human skull."

Smith leaned back on the chair across from Grayson, tonguing the unlit cigarette while glancing at me. "Where'd you find it? In the ice machine?"

"Why would you think she found it there?" asked Molly. Her eyes narrowed. "Seems oddly specific."

I claimed the open seat next to Smith. "It was by

the dumpster. I found it while taking the trash out last night, but now it's gone."

"Don't look at me." Smith lifted his hands in a surrendering pose. "I haven't thrown anyone in the trash."

"This isn't an official investigation as of now," Grayson explained. "I merely wanted to ask if it's possible to trace one of your employee's security cards back to its owner."

"What does an employee card have to do with the skull?" Smith asked.

"I found one underneath the skull," I told him with a shiver. "It seems logical it belonged to someone who worked here."

Smith's jaw tightened as Beckett handed him a copper mug embellished with blueberries and a lime wedge. He spat the cigarette out. "The skull or the card?"

"Both," Grayson and I chorused.

"My employees lose their cards all the damn time," Smith's scratchy voice rumbled. He side-eyed Molly and me. "There must be hundreds of them all over the island." We both briefly averted our gazes away as he took a sip of his blueberry mule.

Grayson retrieved the bagged card from his pocket. "Zoey thought this one looked old. And based on her description, the human remains could be anywhere from five to ten years old."

Smith let out a deep *hmph* and set his mug on the table. He removed his sunglasses to inspect the card closer. In their nests of wrinkles, his gray eyes rolled over to Grayson. "In that case, there's a good chance I know who they both belong to."

FOUR

"I knew it!" Beckett howled, slapping Smith's back. "You *totally* fit the stereotype of a serial killer! I'll bet you're always reminiscing about your 'world tour' because you spent it murdering unsuspecting fans in every city!"

"It's always the ones you least expect," Molly agreed. She draped her enormous melons on Smith and patted the top of his head.

"Would you two fools pipe down?" Smith snapped, jerking away from her. "I haven't murdered anyone. At least *not yet*."

My legs jiggled beneath the table. "Quit drawing it out," I told him. "I need to know."

"I've only had one employee up and leave without any explanation, and she never returned her card."

He took a deep breath while scratching his stubble. "Five or six years ago, a girl by the name of Ginny Jones didn't show up for her shift. I didn't think much of it at the time. She was a young, pretty thing, and a little on the wild side. I just figured she'd moved on. Didn't give it much thought until now."

"That name *totally* sounds made up." Molly rolled her eyes. "She was probably on the lam."

"Can you guess a more specific time frame?" Grayson asked, eyebrows lifted. "Was it summer? Winter?"

Smith chuckled and took a long pull of his mule. "Son, it's always summertime around here."

Grayson briefly glanced away while scratching his chin. "Did you try to contact anyone from her emergency list? Her parents? Friends?"

Taking another sip, Smith shrugged one shoulder. "She never listed anyone. Didn't talk about family or friends either, so I assumed she didn't have any. She was a drifter...didn't have references and didn't give me her social security number. I gave her a trial run before telling her she was hired. If she up and died, it would explain why I never heard from her again."

Beckett paced back and forth with an intense look. "It doesn't explain how her *head* ended up on the property," he pointed out. "Unless someone who worked here whacked her."

"Or someone who *owned* the place," Molly added, throwing Smith a suspicious glare.

I shook my head. "It could've been *anyone* on the island."

"The skull or the murderer?" Smith asked.

"Both," Grayson and I answered together.

"Let's not jump to any conclusions," Grayson instructed my crew, holding the palm of one hand up. "If Smith can somehow confirm the card belonged to this Miss Jones, we can make an attempt to locate her."

"Only active employees are still programmed into the system," Smith told him. With a weighted sigh, he ruffled his short hair. "I'd have to send it into the security company."

Excitement from finding the missing skull and wanting to solve the mystery behind it fizzled. What if that process took weeks, or even months? I had expected a full-on *Law & Order* type of investigation to be launched—the kind where Olivia Benson solves the crime in just one episode. "What do we do until then?" I asked Grayson.

His expression became stern. "We try to locate the remainder of the body."

I REPORTED to work an hour early that afternoon to watch as Grayson, along with Chief Shaw and Deputy Hughes, secured the scene with yellow police tape, and began to dig around the dumpster.

Chief Shaw was several inches shorter than Grayson, and built like an Army tank. With icy blue eyes, buzzed strawberry blond hair, and a gruff demeanor, he would've made an excellent drill sergeant. He even made the standard police uniform of black pants, a white button-down, and black tie look military issued. But he had recently celebrated his 30th birthday at a surprise party his wife had thrown at Beach Bummers, so I knew he could occasionally let loose and have a good time.

Deputy Hughes was closer to Grayson's height, and could've blown straight into the Gulf with a light breeze. The waistline of his pants sagged and the button-down uniform hung from his shoulders the way it would on an actual skeleton. The lifelong local's narrow face and friendly hazel eyes projected a "cute little brother next door" kind of vibe.

With time, a crowd began to gather. Molly did her best to assure gawking guests that everything was okay. I was more interested in watching Grayson, and hoped it wouldn't be long before he ditched his shirt spotted with sweat marks. In the unforgiving heat, his complexion had taken on the shade of a beet.

"We're a little short on waitresses, ladies," Beckett sang, stepping in between us. He draped his arms over our shoulders. "Suppose I could interest you in doing your job instead of leering at the new detective?"

When Grayson leaned on his shovel and wiped his sweaty head with his tattooed forearm, both Molly and I let out quiet hums.

"He looks hot," I commented.

With a repetitive nod, Molly fanned herself. "He sure does."

I slid out from beneath Beckett's arm. "I'm going to get them a pitcher of lemonade."

"You're not on the clock yet." Molly clicked her tongue and pushed me aside. "*I'll* do it."

"Don't even think about sinking your hooks into that one, Molly McGregor," Beckett scolded, stopping her with one hand. "Zoey's destined to bear that man's beautiful babies. Why else would God have put a skull back here for her to find at the exact same time as a new detective moved to the island?"

"You have a point," I agreed, facing Molly with my

arms crossed. "You're always on my case about finding a man. If he is in fact single and would even entertain the idea of going on a date with me, will you *please* stop trying to seduce him?"

Beckett released a scandalous gasp. "Hold on. You don't know whether or not he's spoken for?"

With a snort, I waved my hands through the air. "I just met him a few hours ago!"

"And here I'd already picked out names for your children." Beckett rolled his eyes with dramatic flair. "Wait here. I'll get the lemonade and glasses. Then you're going to take your cute little butt over there and ask him if he's single. If he's unattached, you'll proceed to ask him to take you out dancing."

"In front of his coworkers?" My eyes grew wide. "While he's digging for *a body*?"

With a silent confirmation reflected in his stare, Beckett marched away.

Molly yanked my purple floral shirt out from my shorts.

"What are you *doing*?" I spat, glancing between the crime scene and my friend. "I'm not going to fight you for this guy, Mol. We both know you'd win anyway."

"Stop being so dramatic. I'm increasing your odds." She tied the fabric into a knot in the same fashion she wore her own shirt. "There's no question this man will be interested once he gets a proper preview of your abs. You have a great body, girlfriend. I'll never understand why you don't flaunt it."

By the time Molly was done fussing with my hair and uniform, Beckett had returned with the refreshments. He passed the tray into my sweaty grip. "Have at it, baby girl. Don't forget to bat your eyelashes while giving him your best smile."

"And sway your hips back and forth when you walk," Molly added, nudging me in the direction of the police crew. "Go get 'im, Temptress!"

Because my flirting skills were on the rusty side, I took their advice to heart. By the time I reached the line of yellow tape, I feared Grayson would think I had spent the earlier part of the afternoon getting hammered based on the exaggerated way I was moving my hips and blinking my eyes.

A handful of feet away, the toe of my sneaker caught on a pile of dirt. As I imagined myself landing face first in the grave they'd dug, I shrieked.

Grayson caught my elbow just in time, keeping both me and the tray upright. "Whoa! Careful!"

Looking into his chocolatey eyes, my cheeks warmed. "I thought maybe...uh...you look a little overheated."

"His thin California skin can't handle this humidity," Chief Shaw commented with a deep chuckle. His bear-like grip reached for one of the glasses on the tray and he smiled as I filled it with lemonade. "Thanks, Zoey. That's mighty thoughtful of you."

"Yeah, thanks, Zoey," Deputy Hughes parroted with a broad smile as he retrieved a glass and waited for it to be filled. "Sure is good to see you again."

"No luck?" I asked Grayson as I filled the glass he'd retrieved.

He glanced back at the piles of dirt behind them. "We haven't found anything to suggest a body was ever buried here. Not a single scrap of clothing or other human remains."

With a rush of disappointment, I returned the pitcher to the tray. "I still don't understand why I only found that poor soul's skull. Where's the rest of their body?"

"Are you certain it was a real skull?" Chief Shaw asked with a deep frown. "You kids have been known to indulge in a few cocktails during your shift."

"*Yes*, it was real, and *no* I wasn't drinking." My insides vibrated with irritation. "Why doesn't anyone around here believe me? I swear a human skull was *right where we're standing* only hours ago!"

Grayson's warm fingers wrapped around my forearm. "*I* believe you."

With a steady breath, I squeezed my eyes shut. "There's no way it was fake." Again, I met Grayson's kind gaze. "When you work for someone convinced they were a pirate in another life, you see a lot of plastic replicas. There were way too many flawed details on this one, and it was rock hard."

Deputy Hughes sniggered. "You touched it?"

"I knocked on it," I confirmed through clenched teeth.

The waif-like deputy laughed. "You *knocked* on it?"

"Have you ever knocked on a real skull?" I asked. "Bone is incredibly *dense,* Deputy." *Like your head,* I wanted to add.

"She says it was real," Grayson told the deputy. "No reason not to believe her."

Chief Shaw squinted beyond them to the crowd. "There's not a whole lot we can do without that skull or any other evidence to prove a crime was committed."

I blew a loose red curl away from my face. "I just *know* something bad happened here, Chief. Doesn't intuition count for anything?"

"Not in this situation." He paused to guzzle the last of his drink. "We'll give it another hour or so.

After that, I can't spare any more of my men's time on a fool's errand." He gave Grayson a pointed look. "We can't waste taxpayers' money by investigating intuitions."

My shoulders sagged as I watched the chief return his empty glass. Deputy Hughes gulped his down a moment later, throwing me an uncoordinated wink that included both eyes when he set his glass beside the chief's. The two men turned to reclaim their shovels and resume digging.

Behind Grayson, Beckett and Molly motioned to me like a pair of lunatics with identical impatient, wide-eyed expressions. My pulse sped as I gently nudged Grayson's elbow. Certainly I was about to humiliate myself.

"Thank you for believing me. You could've decided I had a screw loose when I came to you, rambling on about evil crabs and a laughing skull."

One of his toothpaste-commercial-worthy smiles spread over his lips. "It was actually kind of cute."

Cute? I smiled stiffly despite the irritated growl rising in my throat. "Anyway," I continued, "I was thinking...if you still wanted to come back for dinner after work, it'd be my treat. You know, to thank you for believing me, and for making you go to all this trouble. You can totally bring your girlfriend, too."

Grayson's thick eyebrows shot upright. "My girlfriend?"

A flame licked my cheeks. "Wife? Fiancée?"

"It's just me. And I'll gladly take you up on your offer. It's time I start mingling with the locals." He raised a single eyebrow. "Hey, Zoey?"

Nerves frayed, I licked my lips. "Yeah?"

He jutted his chin downward. "Careful or you'll drop that tray."

Squealing, I corrected my grip at the wrong angle. The empty glasses, pitcher, and my pride shattered at the detective's feet. Heat throbbed in my cheeks as I crouched down to pick up the mess.

"I swear I'm normally not this much of a klutz," I told him, eyes fixed on the shards of broken glass. "I guess I'm a little more shook up about finding a dead person than I realized."

A second later, he was squatting beside me, helping collect pieces to put on the tray. "Despite what the chief said, I don't consider the matter closed. Not by a long shot. And what I do with my *personal* time is none of the taxpayers' business." Taking a hold of my shoulder, he lowered his voice. "You and I will figure this out, Zoey."

Although my pride still buzzed with humiliation, I felt a spark of hope.

FIVE

L ate the next afternoon, I launched items of clothing from my closet with the force of a missile. Everything I owned classified as either "cute" or "adorable," just like my personality.

"Who's there?" Teenie demanded in a voice as squeaky as a rusted hinge. "What are you doing in Zoey's room? I may be old, but I'll kick your booty! I know *ka-ra-te*!"

I peered around the corner to find my 100-pound landlord raising her tiny fists in a fighter's stance. "It's just me, Teenie."

Relief flooded her leathery face. In a purple floral coverup and the yellow floppy hat she wore on her daily trip to the beach, the 82-year-old's overly tanned skin was a stark contrast to her new dentures and snowy white pigtails fastened with rubber bands near her shoulders. Teenie was aware her tanning addiction had become unhealthy. Molly and I had decided she was reckless in everything she did, hoping she'd be reunited with her beloved Ernie sooner.

"What's with the cyclone of clothes?" she asked, scowling. "Don't tell me you saw a rat! I can't deal with a rat in my beautiful home!"

Molly slipped into the room behind Teenie, munching on a Granny Smith apple. Based on her messy dark hair and the fact that she was still wearing her pajamas, I assumed she'd been watching soap operas with Teenie all morning. "What's this about *a rat*?" she squeaked.

"There's no rat," I assured them both. "I'm just trying to find something decent to wear. I was too busy to spend any time with Grayson last night, so he volunteered to stop by after his shift today."

"Hold on." Still chomping on a chunk of apple, Molly grabbed one of my shoulders. "How exactly did he word it? What was the tone of his voice?"

"Who's Grayson?" Teenie pipped. "Is this man making a booty call?"

"What?" I shook my head frantically. "No! I mean...I don't know. All I know is he's coming here to talk about the skull, and I want him to stop looking at me like I'm someone's kid sister."

"Skull?" Teenie gasped. "What skull? Did someone die?"

Flinching with my mistake, I eyed Molly. We didn't need to feed Teenie's already overactive imagination.

"Uh...Zoey found a, um, weird *animal* skull at the bar," Molly told her. "She met a crazy-hot veterinarian that wants to help her identify it."

Teenie's eyebrows, drawn in with a flourishing pencil stroke, lifted in my direction. "You're letting a strange man into the house? What if he has a gun? Or a knife?"

"I promise he's not a serial killer," I said.

"Did he tell you that?" Teenie huffed, folding her thin arms. "Because that's exactly what a serial killer would say!"

With a roll of her eyes, Molly steered Teenie toward the hallway. "You better get going before you miss that sexy young doctor taking his afternoon run on the beach!"

"You're right!" Teenie declared, lighting up with a wide smile. "Lord knows what would happen if I missed out on my daily dose of beautiful man-buns! God bless the person that invented Speedos!"

Her wrinkled lips blew us a kiss. "Toot-a-loo, ladies! Don't do anything I wouldn't!"

"That doesn't leave much!" Molly called after her.

Once they were alone, I threw Molly an accusatory scowl. "Why haven't you ever told me I have the wardrobe of a twelve-year old?"

"I have," Molly replied in a dry tone. "Probably a thousand and one times since we've met. Until now, you've refused to listen."

Muttering underneath my breath, I snagged a sundress off the floor and held it out between us. "*Yellow flowers*, Mol. Do you know who wears dresses with yellow flowers?"

"Psychopaths who suddenly realize their wardrobe is lacking in allure?" Molly grabbed the sundress, giggling. "What you need is a tight pair of jeans and a cute crop top to go with those killer heels I gave you for Christmas."

I cupped my chest, frowning. "What I *really* need is a bigger chest."

"Your boobs are perfectly proportionate to the rest of you, Zo. You have Barbie's waist. If you also had her boobs, you'd fall over." Clicking her tongue, Molly snatched my hand and dragged me out from the closet. "We're swinging by the bar to get our paychecks, then we'll find you a killer outfit *and* a push-up bra that'll unhinge that hot detective's jaw."

With the visual of Grayson's jaw dropping, I recoiled. It made me think of the laughing skull.

AT BEACH BUMMERS, a row of shirtless male guests of all ages lined one side of the tiki bar, engaged in a lively debate with Finn, everyone's favorite bartender. The former Minnesota college quarterback had lost his scholarship his sophomore year after suffering from three concussions in a row. Like myself, he'd wanted a break from his shattered dreams and had moved to the island on a whim. In the eight years since, he became a local superstar. Between his small-town charm, impressive athletic build, and All-American appearance, he was the bar's male equivalent of Molly.

"Women these days don't think that way!" Finn insisted, shaking his head of thick, sandy hair. His bright sapphire eyes sparkled when he saw us approaching. "Ladies! Come settle this argument!"

Molly sauntered toward them, full chest on display beneath a spaghetti-strap tank top, thick lashes fluttering. She'd tried numerous times to hook up with Finn, but he'd always deflected her advances. "What's up, handsome?"

Finn braced one arm against the bar. "If a rich, attractive man told you he'd take care of you so you never had to work another day in your life, would you take him up on the offer?"

"Hell no," Molly declared. "I can take care of myself, thank you very much."

"See?" Finn told the men, puffing his chest out. "It's like I told you—the ladies prefer broke guys over rich dudes. Tell them you live in a van on the beach, and they'll go *nuts*."

"Where are you getting your information?" I scolded. "Most women only care about love."

"What does love have to do with anything?" one of the men asked. The rest of his crew howled with laughter.

Molly turned her back on them, rolling her eyes. "Can you please whip up two top-shelf margaritas, Finnster?" She swatted my rear. "I'll duck inside and grab our checks."

As she headed toward the resort, I clambered onto the stool farthest away from the male guests. "Hey, Finn. Do you remember a waitress named Ginny Jones?"

Retrieving a set of colorful margarita glasses with

one hand, he scratched his chin with the other. "Skinny blonde with weird eyes and a big rack, right?"

With the memory of Todd the Terrible's busty cheerleader, I crossed my arms and huffed. "What is it with men and boobs?"

"How can you blame us?" He flashed a dimpled grin as he rimmed each of the glasses with lime juice, then salt. "They're our first source of comfort when we come into the world."

"Same with women, but you don't see *us* obsessing over them."

"Sure you do. You just don't think about them as much because you get to walk around with a pair to admire twenty-four seven."

Rubbing my face with both hands, I groaned. It wasn't surprising that Finn remained single. I watched as he filled the glasses with chunks of ice. "Is there anything *helpful* you can tell me about Ginny? Do you remember her talking about a significant other, or family members? Did she ever mention where she was from?"

"I hope she didn't have a man somewhere, because we went a few rounds. She hooked up with guests all the time too." His eyes narrowed as he poured the expensive tequila. "Can't say I remember her saying anything about family, except the one time she mentioned she had a super rich grandpa. The only time I remember her taking a vacation, she went to visit him."

"Did she mention where he lived?"

"Something with a D." Drumming his fingers against the oak bar top, he rolled his eyes around. "Maybe Denver? Dallas? Detroit? Or was it Duluth? I dunno. I just remember it was some big city."

"Do you remember her talking about leaving the island before she disappeared?"

"How do you expect me to recall *anything*?" He tapped his temple. "I'm here because my brain got knocked around too many times, remember?" He placed the margaritas in front of me. "What's with all the questions about Ginny?"

Stirring one of the drinks with a flamingo-shaped stick, I leaned in closer and lowered my voice. "Did you hear about the skull I found out back?"

His blue eyes bulged. "A *human* skull?"

"No, a pterodactyl's," I deadpanned.

"What does that have to do with Ginny?" he asked, frowning.

"I was hoping maybe she knew something about paleontology."

He scratched his head and glanced around the bar

as Sasha, the oldest waitress at Beach Bummers, approached. Born and raised in Atlanta, she was a true southern belle. According to her stories, she'd remained chaste until twenty-five when she married a family friend's successful son, and gave him four children. While on a family trip to the island 15 years prior, Sasha discovered her husband had been unfaithful to their marriage for years. She promptly sent him back to Atlanta and stayed on the island to raise their children on her own while juggling several jobs. She'd waitressed at Beach Bummers ever since Smith had taken over.

She tossed an order ticket at Finn. "Either there's a full moon tonight, or the heat's makin' the tourists act extra funny." Her flawless red nails patted her white-blond cloud of hair that never seemed to move. "One of them was askin' about a human head found by the dumpster."

"It was a *dinosaur's* head," Finn informed her before sulking away with the long list of drinks.

With a cackling laugh, Sasha murmured, "Bless his heart." With a bright grin, she turned to me. "That one's as odd as a two-headed gator."

"Hey, Sasha, do you remember Ginny Jones?"

"Of course I remember Ginny, sugar." Sasha held a hand beside her mouth and whispered, "I'll never understand how a sweet little thing like her was born with naturally ginormous ta-tas. She swore up and down they were real."

With an unbelieving shake of my head, I let out a sharp sigh. "Do you remember anything *other* than her boobs?"

"Let me think." Sasha tapped her chin before her hazel eyes widened. "Oh! I know! She had goofy eyes just like David Bowie. One was bright blue, and the other looked black because the pupil was much larger. She said she was born that way."

I squeezed the lime into my margarita and took a sip of the sugary goodness. The information about Ginny's eyes was more helpful than hearing about the size of her "ta-tas." I leaned back in the stool, eyeing Sasha thoughtfully. "Did she ever talk to you about anyone in her life, or say where she lived before she came to the island?"

"I think that girl was a loner, bless her heart. She never discussed personal stuff unless she'd gotten up close and personal with a guest, if you get my drift." Sasha folded her arms and grunted. "I didn't care much for that kind of talk, but she told me about it anyway."

"Do you know how old she was?"

"Let me see." Sasha's eyes rolled upward for a

moment. "I believe she'd turned twenty-one just before she moved here. I only remember because I heard her tellin' a guest about the party bus her older sister had rented for the occasion before she'd left home."

"Did she mention a rich grandfather?"

"Not that I can recall."

"Did you know she was planning to leave the island?"

"No, and I couldn't believe it when she just up and left without tellin' a soul. Guess that's how you do things when you're a loner." As a boisterous group of five couples claimed one of the tables, Sasha patted my arm. "I better get back at it. Nice chattin' with you, sweetheart. Enjoy the rest of your day off."

Molly returned just then, tossing a sealed enve-lope in front of me before snagging the untouched margarita. "Drink up, my friend. We've got ourselves some serious shopping to do." Grinning from ear-to-ear, she clinked her glass with mine. "Smith had an exceptionally successful week, and we're reaping in the benefits."

I drank reluctantly, wishing I was home on my laptop. With the information I'd gathered from my coworkers, the desire to search for Ginny Jones had grown even stronger.

AS I PREPARED for my big night with Grayson, I heard a persistent whine outside my bedroom window. I didn't think any of our neighbors owned a dog, and couldn't imagine why one would be in the area unless it had slipped away from its leash. If I hadn't been dressed to kill, I would've gone outside to make sure it was okay.

"Go home!" I yelled out the window.

I spritzed perfume on my pulse points behind my ears and checked my reflection one last time, feeling a fresh rush of nerves. Molly had transformed my unruly curls into sleek waves that spilled past the V of the floral halter top I'd found at my favorite boutique downtown. The strapless bra I purchased with it enhanced my chest an entire cup size. My freckles were nowhere to be seen beneath a dusting of high-end foundation, and the curve of my average lips popped with an application of velvety red lipstick. I didn't care much for the false eyelashes that made me skittish with every heavily-shadowed wink.

When the doorbell rang several minutes later, my confidence vanished. I wished either Molly or Teenie had been around so I had a wing-woman. I admired my butt in my favorite spandex jeans before marching to the front door in a pair of black stilettos.

Breath held, I swung the door open. The expression of surprise that lit Grayson's face warmed my skin like a steak on an open flame. He was extra dreamy in a crisp white dress shirt rolled to his elbows, tan khaki shorts with tan loafers, dark flow freshly combed back. He wet his lips as his eyes lazily took every bit of me in. "Wow, Zoey. You look—"

A blur of black fur charged at him, knocking him off his feet. With a surprised cry, he tumbled sideways into Teenie's favorite hibiscus bush.

"Grayson!" I shrieked, wobbling down the steps to his side.

"Down, boy!" he pleaded among a chuckle, attempting to escape the long pink tongue lapping his face as he sat upright. A medium-sized dog stood over him, whimpering between licks. Between the canine's long nose and straight black coat covered in sand, it appeared to be some sort of Labrador mix. The poor thing's ribs were visible, and it was favoring a front leg. I nearly melted when his massive brown eyes rolled over to me.

"I think he's hurt," I told Grayson.

He pushed up to his feet, bending to scratch the

dog behind the ear while assessing its injury. "You're right. This leg is swollen and there's a lot of dried blood. Poor guy. We better take him to the animal hospital." He began to unbutton his shirt.

My eyes bulged once his tanned, fit chest was revealed. The reality put my previous fantasy of him in swim trunks to shame. The guy was buff in a way that put *Liam Hemsworth* to shame. "What are you doing?" I choked out.

"I just picked this up from the dry cleaner today," he explained with a wink. "Wouldn't want to get it dirty." He handed the shirt to me and carefully scooped the dog off the ground. "There's a blanket in the back of my Bronco. Do you mind spreading it out for him?"

Dazzled, I removed the stilettos from my feet and scooped them up before starting for his vehicle. The way my heart fluttered, I didn't trust myself not to fall.

SIX

While the elderly veterinarian and a young tech examined the dog in the back, I waited in the pet hospital's small lobby alongside a young woman clutching a Chinese water dragon in her arms. I positioned myself as far away from the woman and her peculiar pet as the little room would allow, deciding I didn't care for lizards any more than I cared for aquatic creatures with googly eyes and an overabundance of legs.

Grayson, having stepped outside to call the station, returned to my side a handful of minutes later. "I spoke with animal control," he reported. "If no one steps forward to claim the dog, they'll come retrieve him once the vet clears him for release."

I sprang to my bare feet, relieved when it created a safer distance between me and the green lizard's searching tongue. "And then what?"

"Then they'll take him to the humane society."

The door behind us creaked open. We turned to face the hunchbacked veterinarian swallowed by an oversized white lab coat. "The penetration mark on his leg appears to be from the barb of a stingray," the man told us in a bored tone, adjusting his thick-rimmed glasses when they slid down his hooked nose. "The wound is deep and has become badly infected. Either the leg will have to be amputated, or the animal should be put down to spare him the pain."

Tears thickened my throat. "But we don't know who the dog belongs to," I reminded him.

"More than likely, he was abandoned a while ago," the vet replied. "I doubt he's had a good meal in over a week."

"Would he adjust well to a missing leg?" Grayson asked.

The elderly man waved a thin, darkly veined hand through the air. "Over time, most dogs that undergo an amputation hardly remember they had an extra leg to begin with. This one appears to be quite young. I imagine he'll acclimate just fine, without any difficulties."

"Go ahead with the amputation," Grayson decided. "If the dog's owners aren't found, I'll take care of the bill."

I threw him a baffled look. "Really?"

"That's mighty kind of you, Detective," the vet said with a pleased smile, shaking Grayson's hand. "I'll have the tech inform you when he's ready to be picked up. If all goes well, it should only be a day or two. If you're not interested in taking him in, well, I suppose the humane society will have to find a foster home." He tipped his chin in my direction before addressing the young woman and her lizard. "I'm afraid it's going to be a while yet, Darlene, but I can assure you Lizzy looks perfectly healthy, and *not* ready to 'keel over' as you stated."

With a nearly silent chuckle, Grayson turned to me once we were alone. "Let's go see what we can do to find Ginny."

SITTING BAREFOOT and cross-legged on the living room couch, glass of white wine in hand, I scanned over the notes I had scribbled. "This should be everything Finn and Sasha told me." I tossed the notebook over to where Grayson sat on the floor across from me.

Once he was done scanning the list, he lifted a brow in my direction. "Large '*ta-tas*'?"

"Those were Sasha's exact words." Mortified, I leaned forward to sip my wine, veiling my burning face with my hair. "They must be...uh...impressive, because it's one of the first things Finn remembered about her too."

"Sounds like they've never been to southern California," Grayson remarked with a deep chuckle. Stretching his long, lean legs over the carpet, he leaned back against the base of the arm chair and wiggled his bare toes as he typed into my laptop. "There are more Ginny Joneses on social media than one would think." He slid his fingers over the mouse pad. "Come over here and look at this."

I padded across the carpet with my wine glass still in hand and lowered at his side, doing my best to pretend I wasn't affected by the sharp scent of his sandalwood cologne. He balanced the laptop on his open palm between us. When he kept scrolling, I balked at the screen. "Either the name Virginia was crazy popular among the Joneses, or there are a lot of women on the lam," I commented. "Can't you just run a quick search at the station for missing women?"

He shot me a scolding glance. "The chief made it clear he doesn't want me spending time on this. That means he wouldn't want me using official resources either."

"I guess," I agreed with heavy reluctance.

"Besides, half of these women will be easy to rule out based on estimated age. If your friends are right, our Ginny would be around twenty-seven by now."

I clicked my tongue against the roof of my mouth. "Didn't your mother teach you not to judge a woman based on her looks? Besides, sometimes profile pictures are a way for people to brag about their kids, or honor a deceased family member."

"Valid point." He slid the mouse over to the home button, ready to click. "What about you? Whose picture will I find if I click on your account?"

"You just wanna stalk my profile." With a coy smirk, I snatched the laptop away from him. "Go ahead and ask me whatever it is you want to know."

"What's your family situation? Parents? Siblings?"

"Only child, Dad left when I was too young to remember him. My mom's pretty normal, but we're not that close. Boring stuff. I don't have any horrifying secrets."

His eyebrows jetted upward. "Boyfriend?"

"There was one for many years, and *he* was horrifying. Looking back, I'm relieved he left me for someone else. Marrying him would've been a massive mistake. For starters, I would've been stuck in the Midwest, dodging blizzards every winter." I jabbed the crook of his arm. "Your turn, mister."

"I also have one horrifying ex." He reached for his glass of wine on the canary yellow end table behind him and took a healthy swig. "We were actually married when she left me for someone with a bigger bank account. My last serious ex, the one I thought was the end game, wasn't so horrifying. She was actually the exact opposite. We just wanted different things." Blowing out a long breath, he ran a hand through his hair. "I'm also an only child, but my parents aren't so normal. My mom's a little...intense."

"No kids?" I asked, mentally crossing my fingers.

"None." He sounded relieved.

I caught my bottom lip between my teeth. I felt a tug of envy when he mentioned his last ex was the opposite of horrifying. Did that mean he wasn't over her? It was too deep of a conversation for a non-date. "Wow...an ex-wife." I flashed him a wavering smile. "Is it rude to ask a guy his age?"

"I'll be thirty in March."

Six years older, I thought with a firm swallow of wine. Another flicker of irritation followed. It explained why he regarded me as someone's kid sister.

He motioned to my glass. "I'm trying to think of a polite way to ask whether or not I should be concerned that you're drinking."

Irritation simmered in my gut. *He was worried I was under twenty-one.* "I'm well beyond legal." I wanted to scream into a pillow. "It's these stupid freckles," I grumbled, pointing at my face.

"They're not stupid," he insisted. "They're cute."

There was that word again.

The front door creaked open and slammed shut. "Is this the veterinarian?" Teenie's ancient voice called out. Hardly a moment later, she had scampered into the living room to join us, dousing the room in her peach-scented lotion. I guessed her white t-shirt featuring Elvis Presley and faded denim mini skirt had been purchased many decades prior. The pink flip flops adorned with gemstones, however, were something she had bedazzled herself the week before. Beneath a thick layer of blue eyeshadow, she regarded Grayson with a hard look. "You better not be planning anything sinister with this girl. I still have my Ernie's pistol, and I know how to use it!"

"Teenie!" I scolded.

"I'm actually a police detective with no intention of hurting Zoey." With a silent chuckle, Grayson clambered to his feet. He set his glass of wine down before he stuck out his hand. "Grayson Rivers, ma'am. You must be Zoey's landlord."

Her small, weathered hand disappeared inside of his. She pumped his hand once before her gaze swung over to me. "What happened to the fella that was going to check out that skull you found? And what on earth are you wearing? Are you in some kind of trouble? Did *you* do something sinister?" Her pink fingernails spread over her chest, and her collection of gold bracelets clattered down her bony elbow. "My lord, they're right. It's never the ones you expect."

"Grayson is here as a *friend*, Teenie." I rose to my feet beside Grayson, half-tempted to ask him to leave before Teenie said something devastating. "What are you doing home already? I thought you had cards tonight."

"Agatha served up a bad batch of shrimp." Her tone dropped with a scandalous whisper. "Everyone was rushing to use the toilet except me. Guess it's a good thing I don't like cold shrimp." Her tiny hands waved through the air. "Well anyway, I suppose I'll do the polite thing, and give the two of you some privacy." She poked her finger into the center of Grayson's chest. "Now that I know your name, *Detective* Rivers, you best be on your absolute best behavior. That means if you decide you'd like to be more than friends and get a little freaky tiki with my Zoey, you better use protection."

I gasped, my face in flames. "Teenie!"

Flashing her dentures with a bright smile, Teenie's thin shoulders lifted. "I'm just saying. I was your age once."

Uttering a groan through gritted teeth, I told her, "Good night, Teenie."

"Buenas noches, amigos," Teenie returned.

A deep laugh rumbled in Grayson's chest. "It was nice meeting you."

Blowing him a kiss, Teenie waltzed back to the master suite at the other end of the house, humming beneath her breath. Meanwhile, I chugged what was left of my wine and reached for the bottle to pour another glass.

"She seems like a lot of fun," Grayson commented, his voice still thick with humor.

On any other night, I might've agreed. "I need

MOSCOW MULES & MURDER   73

another job so I can afford my own place," I muttered. "I'm so sorry about her."

"Don't be. I'm not." He reclaimed his glass of wine, taking a quick sip. "What was that about someone coming to check out the skull?"

"Molly made up a story about a veterinarian coming to look at an animal skull. We couldn't tell her the truth. You probably noticed Teenie's paranoid about murder the way it is. She worries on a daily basis that either Molly or I will get hacked into pieces. I'd appreciate it if you'd be careful what you say around her." Cradling my wine glass, I sunk back down to grab my laptop and scrolled back to the list of Ginnys. "We better get down to business. This list is longer than the usual line at Dee Dee's."

Grayson set his glass back down on the end table, then sat and draped his arm on the chair cushion behind me. "Before we go any further, I need to tell you something."

The pounding of my nervous heart vibrated against my eardrums. As his eyes held mine, gleaming with seriousness, I blamed Teenie for making a perfectly pleasant night awkward.

"I imagine finding a human skull was pretty trau-matic for someone outside of my line of work," his deep voice lulled. "But sometimes murders don't get solved, and missing women aren't found. Other times it just takes a lot longer than you'd imagine. Don't let the search for Ginny, or *whoever* this person may have been, consume your life. I've watched far less important mysteries go unsolved, destroying good people in the process. I sense you're a good kid with a lot of heart, and I couldn't stand to watch you break." He gently patted the top of my perfectly styled hair like I was a toddler. "If you ever need someone to talk to, whether it be during the middle of a weekday while I'm at work, or in the dead of night, I'm here to listen. Think of me as the big brother you never had."

Big brother. With a flicker of annoyance, I forced a tight smile. "Good to know. Thanks."

Swiping the notebook back off the floor, he set it in his lap. "I say we start our search with Ginny Joneses in big cities that start with a 'D' and go from there." He unbuttoned the cuffs of his shirt sleeves and rolled them up to his elbows, exposing the start of his yummy sleeve tattoo. "Then we should post something online about the dog to see if anyone's looking for him. Unless we find his owners before he's released, it looks like I'm going to have to learn how to care for a pet post-amputation."

SEVEN

I didn't hear from Grayson while I pulled double shifts at the tiki bar over the weekend. I was grateful for the distance as it gave me time to lick my bruised ego and reprogram my mindset. I stayed busy by making a list of the Ginny Jones accounts we had found, charting whatever information they'd made public, and narrowing the list even further. I decided I'd take the high road, and accept Grayson's friendship and his assistance to find Ginny if that's all he wanted.

Monday evening, right after I'd returned home from work to start a game of gin rummy with Molly and Teenie, my phone buzzed with a call from Grayson.

"What's that face about?" Teenie demanded after Zoey glanced down at her screen. "Did someone die?"

Molly's eyes narrowed. "It's *him*, isn't it?"

"Him who?" Teenie asked. Then the whites of her eyes grew beneath her dark skin. "The sexy detective? Does he want another booty call?"

I shot them each a narrowed look before slipping out the front door into the warm night. I hurried down the stone path among the pygmy palm trees and sat at the curb, afraid my nosy housemates would try to eavesdrop.

"What's up?" I answered, hoping to sound casual.

"The dog was released this afternoon," his deep voice rumbled. "I brought him to my place. He's a little sleepy from the pain meds, but he's hobbling along pretty well. The vet said he should be fully healed in two or three weeks."

"You should really give him a name," I suggested, tucking a loose lock of hair back beneath my head wrap. "It'll help the two of you bond."

He let out a deep hum. "I'm open to any ideas."

Glancing around the dark neighborhood, I tapped my index finger against my phone. The dog was lucky to have survived a stingray attack, and he was even luckier we'd found him before the poison had spread. "How about 'Lucky'?"

"I think you should stop by and see how he likes it."

I loved the idea of touring his cottage. He had shared the details of how he'd bought the two bedroom gulf-front property sight unseen with the help of his realtor and Chief Shaw. "It's after ten. Don't you have to work in the morning, old man?"

"Don't worry, I won't keep you out past your bedtime," he teased back. "Let me pick you up. I'll give you a cold drink in exchange for your advice on something, and we can do a little more digging into Ginny Jones. I'll give you a ride back when you're ready to call it a night."

Although I was exhausted, I also wanted to see his place and check in on the dog. I ran inside to change into a lacy top and fashionable shorts, then filled my housemates in before waiting beneath the yard light out front. I wasn't going to let Grayson come inside to hear more of Teenie's crazy babbling.

As I sat on the bungalow's front step, something among the landscaping caught my eye. Teenie had spread crushed shells around the palm trees and bushes, then added a sprinkling of rocks painted gold. All at once, I was reminded of the night I had come across the skull.

It moved when I reached for the card, and something inside the jaw had sparkled in the dim light. Something gold.

"A filling!" I exclaimed.

"Zoey!" Grayson called out. "You alright?"

Blinking heavily, I glanced up to find him waiting in his Bronco at the curb. He had removed the truck's doors, providing an unobstructed view of his muscular arm slung over the steering wheel, army green t-shirt with the album cover from Soundgarden's *Superunknown* stretched over his firm pectorals, tanned feet in leather sandals, black wayfarer sunglasses still perched on his head even though it was dark.

"The skull had a shiny tooth," I blurted, running toward him. I climbed into the passenger's side and clicked the seatbelt into place. "I just remembered. It was right in the front. *Gold*. It could've been some kind of filling, right?"

"Possibly," he agreed while veering into the road. "Those can last several decades. That could be a helpful detail in our search."

Butterflies broke out in a choreographed dance

inside my belly when I studied his masculine profile a little more closely. He could pound nails with that chin. "Hi, by the way."

He glanced away from the road to throw me a gorgeous smile. "Hi. How was your day?"

"Successful. I made two hundred dollars in tips off just one table that only stayed for an hour. Bachelor parties are always the most lucrative."

His smile evaporated. "I'd sleep better at night if you'd consider arranging for rides to and from work. I know it isn't far, but any one of those guys could decide to follow you home after your shift." He glanced back my way. "Have you put any more thought into getting pepper spray?"

"I kind of forgot about it," I admitted, wincing.

"I'm getting you some along with a stun gun," he decided with an irritated grunt. "I'd appreciate it if you'd keep them both in your purse at all times."

"Okay." It seemed pointless to argue. Besides, there'd been a few times guests had either been too handsy or had shown too much interest, and I had asked one of my coworkers to give me a ride home.

"I've been looking for someone to watch the dog while I'm on the clock," he announced while turning onto Main Street. "At least until he's healed and getting along better." He lifted a thick brow in my direction. "Any ideas?"

I shrugged. "I can watch him when I'm not at Beach Bummers."

He blinked several times. "Really?"

"I don't see why not. I work the dinner shift for the rest of the week. But I'd have to do it at your place since Teenie doesn't want pets in her house."

"That'd be great." He nodded, deep in thought, jaw flexing. "I could swing by to get you in the morning and give you a ride to the resort, then back home later."

I started to protest that I'd rather run, but pinched my lips together, deciding he was in "big brother" mode.

Once we reached the south end of the island, he parked in the narrow driveway of an aquamarine cottage at the end of a short lane. Although it was outdated, the bright pink shutters and white cedar shakes on the gables matched the island's tropical vibe.

I climbed out of the truck behind him and peeked around the side of the house. The small yard was neatly trimmed up to a small patio in back where a set of pink Adirondack chairs faced the gulf beneath a string of colorful lights.

"If I were you, I'd spend every night on that wicked patio," I told him. "This place is awesome."

He started down the stone path, tilting his head toward the cottage. "You might want to withhold judgment until you see inside." He led me to the front door, unlocking the dead bolt before motioning for me to enter. "Take a deep breath. It was an estate sale, so I bought as is—furniture and all. The previous owner was a hundred and two year-old widow."

I stepped inside and immediately slapped my hands over my mouth. Everything was painted a bright neon color, from the lime green walls and chartreuse appliances in the small galley kitchen to the pink furniture and obnoxious decor hung above it.

"Oh no," I whispered among a giggle. "Have you had any adverse reactions to living here yet? Any nausea? Dizziness?"

"Like I said, it was purchased *sight unseen*." He playfully nudged me as he stepped inside and threw his keys beside a flamingo sculpture on the fuchsia countertop. "I get overwhelmed whenever I try to decide what to change first."

"It's a bit much to take in without your eyes crossing." I slid my fingertips over a mermaid sculpture. "That sweet old widow probably last decorated it back in the nineties when obscene colors were trendy." I eyed the lime green paint and decided the house had a lot of potential. "I'd probably start by cleaning out any decorations you don't want, then giving the place a new coat of paint—or *several* coats if you're going with something lighter."

"Any suggestions for color? I'm planning to replace the appliances and furniture as soon as humanly possible." He started for the outdated refrigerator. "Margarita in a bottle okay?"

"I'll take a margarita any way I can get it." I slowly whirled around the room. "If this was my place, I'd paint everything white. Walls included. Maybe add a touch of gray and navy blue here and there to give it a more masculine feel." I plopped down on the couch and tested the springs while studying the pink wicker chairs and kitchen table. "I don't think you need *all* new furniture. Maybe a new couch that isn't so lumpy. The rest of it appears to be in excellent shape. That table and these chairs would look great if painted a different color."

"This is why I wanted you to come over." He approached me with two bottles of pre-mixed margaritas and a charming smile. He popped the top on one of the bottles and handed it over. "Know anyone on the island who hires out for painting?"

I bit my lip. I had never actually painted a room on my own, but I had once run a roller as part of a community project in high school, and I could really use the extra cash to save up for my own place *and* work on a new wardrobe. *Painting can't be too hard,* I decided. "I could do it," I said, shrugging.

Grayson's eyes popped wide. "You really want to spend all day painting before work?"

"Other than watching Lucky, my weekdays are wide open." Shrugging, I took a sip of the ice cold drink. "Besides, I adore extreme transformations. I'm hooked on those renovation shows." I was also eager to prove to Beckett that I wasn't decoratively challenged. I peered past Grayson to a set of doors beyond the kitchen. "Wait. Where *is* Lucky?"

"Inside his new kennel. The vet suggested I buy one to keep him safe whenever I'm not keeping a close eye on him." Grayson shuffled toward the set of doors. "He's been pretty groggy from the meds." He cracked the left door open and peered inside. The dog's quiet snores drifted from the room. "Out like a light," he confirmed, gently closing the door behind him.

"So much for seeing if he likes his new name... poor guy."

Grayson sat across from me in one of the wicker chairs. "Fair warning, the site of his amputation looks brutal. They gave him one of those pillow cones so he won't try to lick the stitches." He tilted his head back and eyed me thoughtfully. "If you're serious about painting, I'd pay you well. It'd be worth it so I'm not stuck doing it on my down time. I could pick you up in the morning to grab paint from the hardware store before I walk you through the routine of care the vet tech suggested."

"You don't have to be my personal chauffeur," I scolded. "I'm used to taking the Gorilla Bus."

Blowing out a long breath, he ruffled his dark hair. "Truth be told, it makes me uneasy knowing someone might've been murdered only yards from where you work. I don't know the island well enough to agree it's as safe as you say."

"You're starting to sound like Teenie. Besides, I'm sure whoever did it is long gone by now."

His jaw hardened. "Or they're living in plain sight somewhere on the island, knowing they can easily get by with doing it again."

I shivered with the thought.

He started for the kitchen and rifled through the

cupboards. "Why don't you go ahead and enjoy the 'wicked patio' while I grab my computer and some snacks?" he called over his shoulder. "I'll be right behind you."

"Can I help carry something?"

"You've been waiting on people all day." He shooed me away with a flick of his wrist. "Go. I've got it."

I slipped back out the front door, grumbling to myself, "Of course you do." I had finally met a considerate man, and he wanted me to regard him as a brother.

Before rounding the side of the house toward the patio, I froze with the sight of headlights. A dark sports car idled farther down the lane, its engine making a soft purr. I wasn't sure of the make or model, but it was low to the ground with a curved hood and smooth lines. Although I couldn't make out the shadowed profile of the driver, I felt a set of eyes on me.

A lump rose in my throat as Grayson's words repeated in my head. *Or they're living in plain sight somewhere on the island, knowing they can easily get by with doing it again.*

"Can I help you?" I called out, taking a few hesitant steps into the road.

The car quickly reversed down the lane. I continued to watch as it reached the end and abruptly spun around, squealing its tires. The tail-lights quickly disappeared into the darkness.

"Maybe they were lost," I said aloud to no one.

Deep down, I knew that wasn't true.

EIGHT

As promised, Grayson came by early Tuesday morning. We picked out several gallons of paint at the hardware store before he dropped me at his house with the supplies I would need. Between boxing decorations for donations, watching videos online that explained the painting process to beginners, giving Lucky the affection he deserved with his gruesome wound, and prepping the walls, I hadn't so much as picked up a brush before Grayson returned from work.

"It's looking better already," he declared, tossing his keys and a small plastic bag onto the counter.

Sighing, I studied my progress and tucked a wayward curl behind the bandana knotted over my head. "It doesn't feel like I accomplished much.

Lucky was a little distracting." With the sound of his new name, the dog rose from his resting place nearby and ambled close enough to lovingly lick my hand. "You're still a good boy." I bent down to scratch behind his ears. *"Oh yes you are!"*

Grayson chuckled. "Glad to see you two have bonded. He's already moving better, too."

"That's all on him," I declared. "He's a natural when it comes to balancing on three legs."

Grayson scratched the dog behind a floppy ear. "I brought you a stun gun and pepper spray. They're in the bag I brought in with me. Let me know if you have questions on how to use them."

I regarded the bag as if it contained a bomb. I was more afraid I'd accidentally hurt myself before I'd have the courage to turn them on someone else. "I'm sure I can figure it out."

He headed into the kitchen and plucked a bottled craft beer from the ancient fridge. "Do you have time for a drink before you go?"

"I'll never turn down a margarita." I stood with an eyebrow lifted. "Besides, I was hoping to run an idea by you before I head out."

"I'm all ears." Winking, he popped the top on another pre-mixed margarita and handed it to me.

"What if I posted something about Ginny in one

of those local online groups where people sell things? I could ask if anyone who knew her would be willing to meet with me. Maybe she made some friends on the island that kept in touch with her after she left."

After taking a drink of his dark beer, Grayson nodded. "That could work." His expression hardened. "Except for the part where you meet with them in person."

I crinkled my nose. "I hate talking to strangers online. It's so easy to misunderstand typed messages without seeing their expression or hearing the changes in their voice."

"That may be true, but anyone who knew Ginny could be a suspect."

"Good point." I paused to take a swig of the margarita. As I swallowed, my eyes widened. "I know! I could ask them to meet me at Beach Bummers after one of my shifts!"

Grayson nodded half-heartedly. "Only if I'm there too."

With a little laugh, I crossed my arms with my margarita held against my elbow. "Are you sure you don't have any younger siblings? You sure have the role of a bossy big brother perfected."

Grayson chuckled as his phone buzzed inside his

pocket. He retrieved it and frowned at the screen. "It's the chief. Hold on, I'll be back in a second." He answered the phone and stepped into his bedroom, closing the door.

I plopped down on the floor beside Lucky, scratching his neck beneath the pillow cone while taking a long pull of the cold margarita. I glanced around the house, admittedly a bit nervous about starting the paint job.

From inside my handbag, my phone chirped with a new text. I crawled across the floor to snatch it from the table. Once I fished my phone out, my skin pricked with the message stretched across its screen.

She has been dead a long time. Let her rest in peace.

With a shaking hand, I opened the text. It came from a blocked number.

"Zoey?" Grayson asked, all at once standing beside me. "What's wrong?"

"I…uh…just realized I lost track of time," I lied, slipping my phone into my shorts' pocket. There was a good chance Grayson wouldn't let me out of his sight if he saw the text. I snatched the bag from the counter and shot him an apologetic look. "I'm going to be late for work."

Someone out there knew something about the skull that they didn't want me to discover.

———————

I DOVE deep into the renovation of Grayson's home, painting nearly everything in sight over the following days. But it didn't go as smoothly as I had hoped. The first day I knocked over a gallon of paint and spent hours cleaning it off the floor before returning to the hardware store to purchase a new gallon. I considered myself luckier than the dog when Grayson didn't comment on my lack of progress. The second day there was soon more paint on my body than the walls, and Lucky happened to hobble through a full roller tray. By the time I'd taken the extra time to wash the dog without disturbing the site of his amputation, and scrubbed the paint off myself in Grayson's pink shower, I had hardly been any more productive than the day before.

Grayson agreed to come to Beach Bummers on Friday night to meet with anyone who'd answered my post about Ginny on social media. On my breaks, I messaged the Ginny Joneses that had made my list, and corresponded with several men who had responded to my post. Although I was excited to gather more information on Ginny, I knew we may never find out if the skull had been Ginny's unless it resurfaced.

Grayson came for dinner at the tiki bar both nights with Lucky in tow. My friends instantly fell in love with the dog. The second night Sasha presented him with a bandana she'd sewn that matched their uniforms, and we declared Lucky to be the bar's unofficial mascot. Even Smith took a liking to the dog. I was convinced it was only because Lucky drew in a swarm of female guests who fussed over the injured pet.

Late Friday morning, I finished the last wall to remain between Grayson's kitchen and living room. Aside from the outdated appliances that were still awaiting replacements, the rooms were a crisp contrast of white and gray with one contrasting wall in navy. While it dried, I ran downtown to the secondhand store to snag a few canvas paintings of sea shells that added a tasteful pop of color.

I stood in the center of the adjoining rooms to admire my work once it was done, wiping the exhaustion from my face with a dried paint-splattered hand. Lucky hobbled around me in circles.

"Eat your heart out, Beckett Barnett!" I declared

with a prideful smile. "I *do* have a good eye for decorating!"

Lucky agreed with two excited barks.

Since I had an earlier shift that afternoon, I showered in Grayson's bathroom and took the Gorilla Bus to Beach Bummers. Although I tipped Stewy, the driver who never failed to stink like bong residue, extra to allow Lucky to ride along, I suspected it hadn't been necessary the way the young driver had treated Lucky like royalty.

The moment I set my handbag behind the tiki bar, Molly came rushing toward me. "Don't freak out," she pleaded, blue eyes more rounded than usual. "Just know we all think it's kind of weird, but we're here for you. There's no need to panic."

"Telling me not to panic is *making* me panic." I pursed my lips while securing my apron around my waist. "What in the name of all that's holy are you talking about, Mol? Did someone die?" Lucky let out a lazy yawn and laid on his back, waiting to be scratched by someone.

Molly's blue eyes remained somber. She swallowed hard when she pulled a folded white envelope from her back pocket. "This was sitting on the bar when Smith opened up this morning." She handed it to me before lowering to rub Lucky's stomach, eyes still on me.

With slightly trembling hands, I unfolded the blank envelope and pulled out a ripped piece of notebook paper. One sentence was scrawled in black permanent marker.

Tell that nosy redhead to stop looking for Ginny Jones

My heart thumped against my ribs. "Oh." *I was officially panicked.* "Has anyone else seen this note?"

"Smith wanted to call the cops, but I told him you'd tell Grayson." Molly stood, twisting her thin fingers through the ends of her dark ponytail. "He'll know what to do, right?"

Releasing a deep breath, I tucked the note back inside the envelope and stuffed it inside my apron pocket. "I'm *not* telling Grayson. You and Smith aren't going to either."

"But, Zo," Molly insisted, clutching my arm. "It could be a note from that woman's *killer*."

"I hope it is. It would mean I'm on the right track."

"I really don't think you should keep this from Grayson. Maybe he could find the person that wrote this by analyzing the handwriting or whatever."

Running her teeth over her bottom lip, Molly scanned the busy bar. "They could be here right now, watching you."

The thought sent a chill racing down my spine. I eyed my handbag, wondering if I should slip the pepper spray inside my pocket. *Just in case.* Instead, I lifted my chin defiantly before my friend could sense my fear. "Good. Maybe they'll be here when I interview everyone about Ginny, and get irritated enough to expose themselves."

I grabbed a stack of menus and hurried past my worried friend to a table of newcomers. I convinced myself that if I stayed busy over the next couple of hours, I wouldn't have time to fret over the fact that someone had been watching me at Grayson's, somehow obtained my phone number, and now they had located me at my place of employment.

───

"YOU HAVE an interesting line up of suitors, baby girl," Beckett informed me as he rounded the corner of the tiki bar with a full tray in hand. "Number six just checked in."

Excitement fluttered in my chest as I peered past Beckett in search of the newcomer. In my post about

Ginny, I had asked anyone who knew her to arrive around eight when I was done with my shift, and they'd started arriving as early as seven. I watched as Grayson rose from a table where the other five men sat to shake the hand of a short, forty-something man with a patch of dark hair in the middle of his wide forehead, and a doughy gut that hung over his zipper. He was nothing like the other twenty to thirty year olds donning respectable collections of tattoos and piercings.

"I sure hope you know what you're doing, Nancy Drew," Beckett grumbled as he started for a table of boisterous college-aged guys.

Molly moved in next to me, shoving her notepad into her apron as she stared at the group of men. She curled her dark ponytail around a finger. "What if one of them turns out to be Ginny's murderer?"

"That's why Grayson insisted on being here," I told her with a little shrug. "It's not like they're going to murder me with dozens of witnesses."

"No, but they might follow you home, and murder us both."

"With Grayson around? Highly unlikely."

As if hearing his name, Grayson turned in my direction and gave a simultaneous grin and nod of his head before returning to the table with the older guy.

"I cannot believe you've been spending all this time helping that beautiful man transform his house, and he hasn't made any kind of move yet." With a dramatic sigh, Molly turned away from where Grayson sat with Ginny's assumed lovers, and started for the bar. "Such a travesty."

"It's not like I asked him to pay me with sexual favors," I scolded, hurrying after her. "Besides, I don't expect him to be making the moves anytime soon. He's made it crystal clear that he sees me as someone young—*naive*—and in need of his protection." I pulled the string on the small waitress apron tied around my waist and removed it. "I know it's not quite eight, but I don't want to miss out on whatever it is they're telling Grayson about Ginny." I shoved the apron into Molly's hands and flashed a nervous smile. "With any luck, maybe we'll find out whether or not Ginny could still be alive."

"*Be careful!*" Molly warned as I started for the group of men. "Tell them you're shacking up with a Navy SEAL or something so they won't mess with us!"

Before I could reach Grayson, Finn snuck in next to me. I couldn't deny he was handsome in a dark button down and slim gray khakis, sandy hair gelled back. "Hey, Zo!" He slung an arm around my neck. "What's poppin', cutie? Busy night?"

"Hey, Finn." He reeked of expensive men's cologne. Enough that I wondered if he had literally bathed in it. I willed my eyes not to roll to the darkening sky. "What are you doing here on your night off? Don't you have a hot date?"

Two middle-aged brunettes in bikini tops and jean shorts strolled past, giggling. Their laughter died on their lips when Finn grinned in their direction. He always had that effect on women.

"Good evening, ladies." His voice was syrupy sweet as he tipped an imaginary hat.

The taller of the two batted her dark lashes. "Well, hello there, handsome."

When they hurried off, giggling and whispering, he turned back to me. "I wanted to stop by because someone online asked for information about Ginny Jones. I figured I could at least let them know she's a dinosaur doctor."

I covered my face with my hands. *Just how hard had he been hit when he'd received those concussions?* I wondered. "I'm the one who posted it, Finn." I almost felt sorry for him when he threw me a confused look.

"But you already asked me about her."

Willing myself patience, I lifted his arm from around my neck. "Why don't you go hang out with Lucky and buy those two women a drink?"

"That doesn't sound like a bad idea," he agreed, peering over to where the women stood beside the bar.

As he shuffled away in the sand, Grayson approached me with an urgent speed, wrapping his fingers around my elbows. "You're just in time."

Heart fluttering from his touch, I took in his sandalwood scent and the sparkle in his chocolate brown eyes. "In time for what?"

His lips spread with a warm smile. "Ginny's brother just arrived."

NINE

I snuck a glance over at the last man to shake Grayson's hand. He was at least two decades older than Ginny, and looked sorely out of place on the beach in black loafers paired with dress pants and a dress shirt the same shade of yellow as the polka dots on his bright green tie. Perspiration lined his forehead as he eyed the other men who had answered my post about Ginny.

"Are you sure he didn't say he's her *dad?*" I whispered to Grayson.

"Didn't your mother teach you not to judge a man based on his looks?" Grayson teased with a short chuckle. "Listen…I'll let the others go, and we can interview the brother together." He glanced back at the motley crew of men chatting at the table behind him. "I'm pretty sure I've extracted all the information I'm going to get out of those guys."

Disappointment loosened my muscles. "Really?" I would lose my chance to draw out whoever had left the note and sent me a text. "What did they say about her?"

"None of them remembered her having a gold tooth or any kind of unusual dental work. I'm convinced half of them only agreed to come here because they thought maybe she was back in town. They basically all said a different version of the same thing—Ginny was an adventurous lover, and had a nice set of—"

"Okay, I get it," I said, stepping back to disconnect his fingers from my elbows. Eyes fluttering to the dark sky, I held out the palms of my hands. "Considering you're a detective and everything, I'll trust your instinct on this."

His smile slipped into a one-sided grin. "Go ahead and grab a smaller table for the three of us. I'll bring the brother over in a minute. You can take the role of lead interrogator."

When he turned away, I peered at the alleged brother one last time. *What if the man was only pretending to be Ginny's brother?* I wondered while snagging one of the high top tables farthest from the tiki bar where it wasn't as loud. *Could he be the one harassing me?*

I jumped when Beckett set a glass of water on the table. Lucky was right on his heels. "Well? Did you find Ginny's killer?"

"No, but apparently we caught the attention of her brother." I bent to straighten Lucky's bandana and offer him my water. His long, pink tongue lapped it greedily. "Hopefully he'll have some helpful information."

"You've been hanging around Detective Dark and Dreamy for an entire week now, Zo. You've redecorated his house, and you're fostering a stray together." Beckett set a fist on his hip and wiggled his eyebrows. "Are you going to sit there and tell me the two of you still haven't done a little tango in the sheets?"

"I already told you guys…he wants me to think of him as a big brother," I muttered, scratching Lucky's fur beneath the pillow cone.

Beckett let out a flat laugh. "Sweetie, this is the South. That never stopped anyone around here." As Grayson and Ginny's brother started for us, Beckett straightened. "Just act cool, and turn up your flirt a notch. I know you have it in you. I'll come back for your drink orders."

In a handful of excited heartbeats, Grayson and the man had joined me. I stood as Grayson made the introductions.

"Zoey Zastrow, meet George Jones."

I shook the man's hand, not surprised to find it cold and clammy considering the amount of sweat on his forehead. "Thank you for coming to meet with us, Mr. Jones."

The man replied with a genuine smile. He was somewhat handsome up close, with a square jaw and sharp, masculine features. "Call me George. And actually, I came here because I was hoping you'd know something about Ginny's whereabouts."

Grayson and I exchanged a quick look of concern before we sat. Lucky sprawled out in the sand beneath my chair with a satisfied groan.

"When did you last see her?" I asked.

In the seat beside me, George rubbed at his forehead and closed his eyes. "Let me see…our sister Ginger last saw her on her twenty-first birthday. I think I last saw her almost an entire year prior to that."

"You hadn't seen her in a year?" I asked.

He glanced back at me and let out a weighted sigh. "I should probably give you a little background on Ginny before you make any judgments. She's a half-sister, born out of our dad's work affair. My sister and I were adults, and our mom was just starting to enjoy empty-nesting. The woman sleeping with our dad was a young nurse at one of the clinics he frequented, and announced she wasn't keeping the baby. She didn't want to be anchored down by a child. When our mom found out, she insisted on raising Ginny as her own."

"Whoa," I whispered. "That's—"

"It wasn't as easy-going as it sounds, believe me," George told me with a *humph*. "She was still very much in love with our dad despite his indiscretions, and she couldn't stand the thought of his child being terminated. Things were a little awkward once they first brought Ginny home from the hospital. My sister and I could sense the tension between our parents. And Ginny came into the world looking like a carbon copy of her birth mom. As she grew older, she had her wild attitude, too. She did pretty much whatever she wanted, and wouldn't listen to anyone. Our mom started to resent her a little more with every year, and eventually moved out. Dad was left to raise a five-year-old by himself with occasional help from our sister Ginger. I lived six hours away with my wife and kids of my own, but Ginger went to college nearby in Niceville, so she was able to drive to Destin on weekends to help watch Ginny."

"You grew up in Destin, Florida?" I asked. *Could it be the 'D' city Finn had vaguely remembered?*

George nodded. "I eventually moved back there once Ginny got older." He slumped back in his chair. "Ginger tried her hardest to be a mother to Ginny, but she eventually resented the role because she was missing out on the college experience. It almost cost me my marriage when I tried to help out. Ginny was so wild that my kids were scared to be around her. Our dad was a pharmaceutical salesman, and spent a lot of time on the road. He hired whatever babysitters he could find to watch Ginny. Most of them weren't fit to care for a child. She basically grew up with an endless string of incompetent strangers watching over her. By the time she was thirteen, she was drinking hard alcohol and smoking weed daily. She dropped out of high school right before her sophomore year to live with some older guy she'd met. That's when we started to lose track of her. Ginger would occasionally see her waitressing at tourist bars." His eyes swept over the property. "I always figured she'd end up working at a similar place, but you have to understand there are thousands of these types of bars in

Florida. Last we'd heard, she had returned to Destin long enough to claim the estate willed to her by her grandfather, and then disappeared again. If I hadn't had an alert set on my phone for her name, we may never have learned what happened to her after she left Destin."

I felt a sudden connection to Ginny. We both had absent fathers. Only I had a fun and loving mom who was one of my best friends, and it sounded like poor Ginny really didn't have anyone. "So you *did* have a wealthy grandfather?"

With a bitter sneer, George let out a flat chuckle. "He wasn't my relation. It was her birth mother's father."

"Do you know the approximate time period in which she returned to Destin to claim that estate?" Grayson asked.

George shook his head. "I'm afraid that's something you'd have to ask my sister, Ginger."

Beckett returned with a mischievous smile. "I already know what this one wants to drink," he said to me. "Always a blueberry mule for my little jewel." He eyed Grayson and George. "What can I get you two gentlemen?"

Grayson tipped his chin. "I'll take one too."

"That sounds delicious," George agreed, setting

the drink menu back in the center of the table. "Put me down for the same."

Beckett winked in my direction. "Anything for Zoey's friends."

When Beckett turned to walk away, George's gaze bounced between mine and Beckett's matching shirts. He tipped his chin at me. "Did you work here with Ginny?"

A lump pushed against my throat. "I didn't start here until several years after she…ah…" I glanced over at Grayson, silently begging for help. How was I supposed to tell the man we suspected his sister was dead?

"She took off without telling anyone where she was going, or even that she was leaving," Grayson explained.

George chuckled softly. "Sounds like Ginny." Then the chuckle died on his lips. "Wait a minute. Why are you looking for her *now* if it's been over five years since she last worked here?"

Grayson folded his hands and cleared his throat. "There's no delicate way to tell you this, George. We have reason to suspect something may have happened to her. Zoey recently stumbled across some evidence that may indicate Ginny was somehow involved."

"You sound like a damn cop," George snapped. His face began to turn a dark shade of scarlet when he glanced between me and Grayson. "Would someone give it to me in straight English?"

I lightly set my hand on George's shoulder. "I found skeletal remains behind the resort. We think they belonged to a woman. There was a Beach Bummers' employee card nearby with an older logo that would fit the time period Ginny worked here."

Letting out a sharp breath, George pinched the bridge of his nose. "I always feared she'd end up dead."

"At this point we're only speculating whether or not it could be your sister," Grayson clarified. "Based on the condition of the skeletal remains Zoey described, the timeframe would coincide with Ginny's disappearance."

"Why didn't the police try to get in touch with me or Ginger?" George demanded. "Have they run dental tests?"

Guilt tugged at my insides. "Because the skull disappeared."

"How does a skull disappear?" he snarled with a scowl. "From police evidence?"

I sunk a little deeper into my chair. "From the spot where I found it."

He let out a dry bark. "You're saying no one else saw this skull except for you? Were you *on drugs*, by chance?"

"Zoey wasn't under the influence of anything," Grayson assured him with an edge of irritation to his voice. "We aren't exactly sure what might've happened. She found the remains one night after working a late shift, and the next morning it was gone. The local PD dug for other remains in the adjacent area, but came up empty-handed."

Heat tingled at the base of my neck. "I think…a, um, crab may have taken off with it."

"Maybe it was a hallucination caused by exhaustion," George huffed, sliding from the chair to stand. "This has *clearly* been a waste of my time. I can't believe I drove all this way just to hear some flaky kid tell me she had a wild theory about my sister being dead without a shred of evidence to prove it!"

"I'm not a kid!" I protested at the exact time Grayson declared, "She's *not* a flake."

George shook a finger in my direction. "I know how you kids like your murder mystery parties and true crime stories, but this is a real human being we're talking about!"

Jaw set, Grayson rose to his feet across from him. "Mr. Jones, you're out of line. You somehow got the wrong impression about Zoey's intentions. She's been relentlessly dedicated to uncovering the identity of this woman even though people like you refuse to take her seriously. I believe you owe her more respect than what you've shown." From the cords of tension in his neck, it seemed he was ready to fight the much smaller man if he didn't comply. "Have a seat," he added in a firm tone, motioning to the empty chair.

The start of a flush burned at the base of my neck. Grayson's sudden burst of aggression on my behalf was incredibly hot. I silently thanked Beckett's timing when he rushed in with our drinks, hopeful the cool liquid would halt my blush.

George hesitated, deciding to reclaim his seat after Beckett placed the copper mugs on the table. He was the first to take a drink. "These are excellent," he declared.

"I know," Beckett sang with pride before leaving.

I regarded George with a kind look. "Whoever that skull belonged to has a family somewhere, probably worried about them the exact same way you and Ginger are worried about Ginny," I explained, my voice gentle. "The only connection we've been able to make without any evidence to go by other than the employee card is the fact that your sister disappeared around the same time. We simply want to rule her out as the victim." I took a quick sip of my mule. "Do you know by chance if Ginny had a gold filling?"

"I don't know much about her medical history," George admitted with a sheepish look. "But Ginger might."

Another pang of disappointment lowered my shoulders. "Could you please ask her and let me know? It was dark, but I swear I saw something sparkle in the skull's mouth that night."

With a nod, George took another long drink from his copper mug. Then he smacked his lips together and said, "I could do that."

As I watched George consume his drink, I let out a hasty breath. I was running out of questions, and didn't feel any closer to discovering Ginny's fate.

With a measured look, Grayson sat back with his arms folded over his chest. "Is there anything else you could tell us that might be helpful in our search for her?"

"Buddy, if I knew something useful, we probably would've found her by now. But if I can think of anything, or if Ginger has something useful to add, I have your number." George sucked from his little blue straw one last time before pushing his drink away. "I better call it a night. I have to drive back early tomorrow for my daughter's dance recital."

I stood to shake his hand. "Thanks again for coming all this way, George."

He gently squeezed my hand before releasing it. "Sorry I reacted the way I did. You have to admit it all sounds a little far-fetched. If you find anything on Ginny, please let us know. Grayson has my number."

I answered with a tight smile and a little nod, then caught Grayson's gaze. "When Beckett returns, order me another mule. I'll be back in ten."

Lucky hobbled behind me as I made my way inside the resort toward the employee bathroom. I hadn't taken a break since I had clocked in for my shift, and my bladder had begun to ache.

Mariah, an always bright-eyed and bushy-tailed blonde, gave a little wave as we passed the front desk. She was nice enough, but I sensed there were kindergartners with more common sense than the 23-year-old from North Dakota. "Hey, Zoey. Hey, Zoey's tripod dog."

I absentmindedly waved back before slipping into the narrow hallway that led to the restrooms and Smith's office. I made it inside the single stall and plopped down on the toilet only seconds before my full bladder decided it was done. I moaned in relief.

Lucky camped out right in front of me and whimpered, begging to be pet.

"And George thought our meeting was a waste of *his* time," I muttered while scratching beneath Lucky's cone. "We're not any closer to finding Ginny than we were five days ago."

All at once, darkness swallowed the room.

"Hey!" I exclaimed, blindly reaching for toilet paper. "Someone's in here!"

A set of heavy footsteps fell over the tiled floor. Then, silence.

"Hello?" I called out, quickly finishing up and wiggling back into my shorts. "Is someone there?"

Sharp breaths came from somewhere in the darkness.

A primal sense of fear gripped the base of my spine as I crouched down, cradling Lucky's head against my stomach. "I have a can of pepper spray in my hand, and I'm not afraid to use it!" she lied. *If only I had slipped it into my pocket earlier when the idea crossed my mind.*

The familiar sound of the broken lock on the stall being slid open sent my stomach tumbling over itself. *Someone was coming for me.*

Far too close by for my comfort and sanity, a raspy voice whispered, "Stop searching for Ginny."

A deep growl of warning vibrated low in Lucky's throat. A moment later, he sprang forward, pushing the door open. A myriad of sounds followed. More growling. A man yelping.

"Lucky!" I cried. Although I was afraid he'd rip his stitches, I was more afraid of the stranger threatening me.

The bathroom door slammed against the wall, and a flicker of the hallway light passed through the room before falling dark again.

I gently pushed on the stall door. "Lucky?"

He answered with a high-pitched, distressed whine. I pressed my back against the wall and carefully shuffled over to the light switch, managing to avoid tripping over Lucky. When I turned on the light, I found him curled into a ball beneath the sink, trying to lick the site of his amputation.

Right outside the bathroom stall, next to several droplets of blood, there was a ballpoint pen that hadn't been there when I had first entered. I bent to inspect the white words printed across the blue pen.

Island Sunshine Rentals
Ron Finkle, Owner/Agent

TEN

The dire looks Grayson kept throwing me on the ride back to his house would've knocked me right off my feet with flattery if I hadn't been so irritated with myself.

"Are you sure you're okay?" he asked as he parked in his driveway.

"I told you, I'm fine," I grumbled, tugging the resort beach towel tight around my shoulders. Either Beckett or Molly had thrown it over me shortly after I had burst outside, yelling for help over the bar's festive reggae music. A majority of the customers seated around the tiki bar had merely regarded me like I was a lunatic, likely too drunk to react to my pleas.

Molly, Grayson, and Beckett had nearly collided

when they came running. They appeared equally concerned as I explained Lucky had attacked someone in the employee bathroom. Grayson then sprinted into the building while my friends stayed behind to console me.

Grayson had quickly emerged with Lucky cradled in his arms. I rode along to the animal hospital where we were assured by the veterinarian on call that Lucky would be just fine after they repaired his stitches. Still, they kept him overnight so he could be monitored for any further injuries they'd missed.

"It's Lucky you should be worried about," I told Grayson, fighting back a sudden rush of tears. "I should've stopped him from charging at the man when he let out a warning growl."

"You did the right thing." With a heavy sigh, he pulled his keys out of the ignition. "You can't step in front of a dog in an aggressive mode. I've seen little kids and grown men with their faces half torn off from doing just that."

"But Lucky isn't aggressive. He was only protecting me."

"It still would've been a bad idea." He stretched his neck to the stars above. "I can't believe the resort's receptionist didn't see anyone else entering or leaving the employee bathroom."

MOSCOW MULES & MURDER   117

"Maybe it's because Mariah has been the recipient of the Darwin award. Numerous times."

"Or maybe the attacker crawled in and out of Smith's window. I'm just glad Lucky was there to protect you." He turned his head to the side, eyes dark in the light of the moon with worry. "I filled the chief in on what happened. He wants you to stop by the station tomorrow to give an official statement. In the meantime, he's going to have the hospital notify him if anyone comes for treatment of a dog bite." Throwing me a friendly smile, he opened his door. "Let's go inside and you walk me through what happened again. No detail is too small."

I lumbered behind him to the house, fingering the pen in my pocket left behind by the whispering man. It could've been something the man picked up from anywhere on the island. Or it could have a direct connection to my stalker.

I hadn't told Grayson about the pen, or the whispered threat—only that Lucky had been attacked. I told myself it was because there hadn't been time. Lucky had needed our immediate attention. Truthfully, however, I dreaded having to disclose every detail, knowing I would be forced to tell him about the note someone had left at the bar, the random text I had received, and the car that had parked across the street from his place. I doubted Grayson would ever let me out of his sight again.

"Whoa!" Grayson shouted from inside.

I froze just outside the cottage doorstep, my heart seizing. *Was someone inside? Had my stalker been waiting for us to return?*

Grayson popped his head through the cracked door. His crooked smile fell from his lips when he saw my fearful expression. "Zoey?"

I lifted a hand to my chest, trying to wrench a lighthearted laugh from my gut. "You were yelling...I guess it scared me."

His brows stitched together. "Sorry. I was just floored by the transformation. I can't believe how great the place looks!"

Moving toward the house, I frowned. "You haven't been home yet?"

"I worked late and went straight to the tiki bar from the station. It's fair to say you exceeded my expectations." He still looked puzzled by my reaction when he offered his hand. "Come on. I owe you way more than a margarita, but it seems like a good place to start."

My feet moved on autopilot as I slipped my hand inside his. The warmth of his touch eased some of my fear as I followed him inside. Then, as he withdrew his hand to close the door behind him, I was struck with the eerie feeling of not having to brace myself for Lucky's affectionate greeting.

"I should've carried the pepper spray in my pocket," I blurted with another rush of tears. "Then I could've fought him off myself. Then maybe Lucky—"

Grayson spun around, quickly folding me in his strong arms. "You heard the vet. Lucky's going to be just fine. It's normal to second guess your reaction after an incident like this, but you did the right thing, Zoey." He squeezed me a little tighter. "As much as I care about that dog, I'm grateful it wasn't *you* I had to take to the hospital tonight." His warm lips briefly pressed against the top of my head. I relaxed into the kiss, wishing his lips were elsewhere.

Then he released me and started walking backward toward the kitchen with a cute little grin. "Since Molly and Beckett are both closing tonight, I told them I'd keep you here until morning. I'll take the lumpy couch, and you can have the bed."

With a sudden sweep of embarrassment, I shook my head. I didn't want to sleep alone in his bed any more than I wanted him to treat me like a kid sister and be kissed on the head. "Grayson, I appreciate the offer, but Teenie's home. I'll be fine."

"You expect me to believe your hundred pound, eighty-something landlord will protect you?" He shook his head, laughing. "There's no point in arguing. Your friends agreed you shouldn't be alone tonight. Do you want to be the one to tell them you wouldn't listen?"

I knew by his determined expression that I had no other choice.

SATURDAY WAS my first day off in a week. Although I had planned to sleep in, I hadn't been able to keep my eyes closed for long once I was engulfed by Grayson's scent and tangled inside his soft cotton sheets, face buried in his feather pillow, bare skin covered by his worn t-shirt featuring a picture of AC/DC's Brian Johnson screaming into a microphone. Being tucked beneath his black comforter and wearing his shirt had brought up feelings he clearly wouldn't reciprocate anytime soon. I wasn't the least bit surprised when I was awake to witness the sun first breaking through his bamboo blinds, exposing the masculine details of his bedroom.

After slipping back into the shorts I'd worn to work the previous night, I padded out into the kitchen. With the delightful sight of Grayson sprawled out on the couch, dark lashes fanning across his strong cheekbones, one impressively muscular leg poking out beneath a navy blanket, dark hair ruffled, I felt an overwhelming urge to bolt. I wasn't equipped with the skills to deal with what felt like "the morning after" when nothing had happened beyond friendly conversation and a few cocktails. Yet I was wearing his shirt and he was half-naked. The situation was equal parts awkward, frustrating, and humiliating.

I quietly collected my belongings and crept outside.

A HIGH-PITCHED TINKLING bell hung above the glass door announced my arrival as I stepped foot inside the small, sleek agency on Main Street. Listings for local rental properties, many which I recognized from my daily run, plastered two walls. A small reception area contained a sleek leather couch and a knee-high cascade fountain with monster-sized koi fish swimming at the bottom. Between the lingering aroma of mango and the easy-going music playing from a blue-tooth speaker, the atmosphere was spa-like.

From inside my pocket, my phone buzzed for the umpteenth time since I had snuck out of Grayson's house. I tugged it out from my pocket to see it was him calling yet *again*. While I had showered and changed at home, he'd left half a dozen voicemail messages. I typed out a message, letting him know I left early because I had several errands to run before he took me to the station to make my statement about the attack.

I nearly dropped my phone with the sound of someone exclaiming in a heavy New York accent, "Hey, I know you! You're that friendly redhead I always see running down Main Street, waving at everyone. Don't you work at Beach Bummers?"

I returned my phone to my pocket and closed the distance between myself and the perky woman behind the glass receptionist's desk. The frizzy-haired blonde wore a turquoise tropical print sundress, paired with a blinding collection of jewelry. Over a heavy application of foundation, her cheek-bones glowed with bronzer.

"That's me. My name's Zoey Zastrow."

The woman pressed her slender hands against

her plump cheeks and released a high-pitched squeal. "Oh my god! *Zoey*! What a perfectly adorable name for a perfectly adorable girl!" She popped up to her jewel-sandaled feet, thrusting her hand out. The petite woman made me feel tall for a change. "I'm Glori....with an 'i.' Pleased to make your acquaintance, sweetheart!"

Long red fingernails poked at my knuckles when we exchanged a quick handshake. "I think I remember seeing you at the bar. Long island iced teas with top-shelf tequila, right?"

Glori pressed the palms of her hands against the sides of her face. "You got me there! You can take a girl out of Long Island, but you can't take Long Island out of the girl!" The woman cackled with laughter. Dozens of bracelets clinked down her arms when she lowered her hands down to her waist. "What can I do you for, Miss Zoey? Ready to upgrade to something oceanside? Maybe something with a little more pizazz?"

"Something like that," I decided. Beyond confronting Ron Finkle to see if he could be my stalker, I hadn't thought the process through. My fingers rolled the ballpoint pen inside my pocket. I needed a solid cover story. "My boyfriend and I are looking to rent a place together, so I'll finally be able to afford an upgrade."

"Oh, how exciting! I remember the first time I rented a place with my husband. It was god awful—an efficiency apartment on the Lower East Side of Manhattan. Smaller than the room we're standing in now. The pipes groaned, the windows leaked whenever it rained, and I'm pretty sure a family of rats lived in the kitchen cabinets, but it was ours." A spark of affection passed through the woman's sharp hazel eyes. "You know what I'm saying?"

"Sounds lovely," I answered, nodding.

"Hold on a minute, sweetheart, and I'll see if Ron's still on his cell phone. He should be able to fit you in before his first appointment, no problem." The woman turned, momentarily disappearing behind a solid white door. I held my breath, wondering if I had made a mistake by confronting the man without telling anyone. But the man stalking me could be anyone on the island. A random pen embossed with Ron Finkle's name didn't mean anything.

I continued to believe that diluted theory until the woman returned a minute later to produce a tall, 50-something man in a gray suit over a white shirt partially unbuttoned. He was reasonably attractive, or so I figured someone my mom's age would decide, sporting full mocha hair and a well-groomed mustache equally speckled with fine silver hairs. Faint lines creased his deeply tanned forehead and feathered around his eyes, hinting he was well past his prime despite the youthful smile with slightly crooked teeth he flashed at his receptionist. I couldn't be sure, but I thought I had also seen him a time or two at Beach Bummers.

Time stopped when the man reached up to brush a lock of wayward hair from his forehead.

His hand was wrapped in a clean white bandage.

I swallowed a whimper as my eyes dragged upward to meet the man's wide-eyed look.

His smile evaporated.

I was certain I was eye-to-eye with my attempted attacker.

ELEVEN

Holding the surprised stare of Ron Finkle, my heart twisted. A painfully drawn-out moment passed before he grimaced and shoved both hands inside his pants' pockets. Would he attack me in front of his irritatingly cheerful receptionist?

Judging by Glori's beaming smile, she was clueless as to the tension I felt. "Ron, this is Zoey Zastrow. She's looking to make an upgrade with her beau. They're shacking up together for the first time. Isn't it romantic?" She touched Ron's arm. "Remember the place we first rented together on the Lower East Side?"

A wave of unease swept through my insides. *Ron and Glori were a couple.* But were they a "Monica and

Chandler" kind of couple, or a "Joker and Harley Quinn" kind of couple?

Ron squared his stance and attempted a smile. "Nice to meet you, Miss Zastrow." His thin lips settled into a hard line. Was he preparing to pounce? Would peppy little Glori be strong enough to help him hide my body?

The bell over the Island Sunshine Rentals' front door announced the arrival of someone behind me. *Saved by the bell,* I realized with a slight shudder.

"Zoey?"

The rumble of Grayson's deep voice knocked the air from my lungs. As hard as I had been crushing on him ever since we first met, I never imagined I could be even more excited to see him than usual. I was safe from Ron. *For now.*

With my back to the potentially murderous couple, I rose to my tiptoes and flung my arms around his neck before brushing a soft kiss across his warm lips. Although my body tingled in celebration of the unplanned kiss, Grayson's arms remained at his sides, and his body stiffened.

Heat prickled my cheeks. If he had responded differently, I might've kissed him again. I was desperate for any excuse to pause the predicament I had placed myself in. While I was certain whatever was beneath Ron's bandaged hand would prove his guilt, I wasn't ready to blindside Grayson with the truth. Besides, I knew he didn't carry his gun when he was off duty, and both Glori and Ron could be dangerous.

When I pulled a still-stunned Grayson tight against me for an embrace, I noticed a dark colored sports car parked around the corner, and swallowed a yelp. "Please, help me out of this," I whispered into his ear. I couldn't stand the thought of looking him in the eye after his cold response. "I need an excuse to leave. I'll explain later."

He finally reciprocated the hug, arms slightly limp with reluctance. Worse yet, his hands patted my back in a condescending manner. I realized a moment too late the lie could create havoc for a newcomer on the island—especially one in the public eye. The pack of gossiping old birds who gathered at Dee Dee's every morning would quickly spread word about the new detective dating someone much younger.

"You must be the boyfriend!" Glori sang excitedly. "My, aren't you a handsome one! Don't they make a striking couple, Ron?"

Grayson slipped his arm around my waist and tucked me against his side before we turned to meet the curious looks of my alleged stalker and his wife. "Sorry to cut this short," he told them. "Zoey forgot we promised to pick my parents up from the airport this morning. If we don't leave now, we'll be late. I'd hate to give them a first bad impression of my girl."

"First time meeting the parents!" Glori clapped her hands together. "How exciting!"

With one eyebrow slightly raised, Ron's dark gaze fell on me. "I was looking forward to meeting with you. I trust you'll make an appointment with my wife for a time that works best with your schedule." Even though his expression remained stoic, I could sense he was projecting a silent threat. I wished he'd whisper so I could decide whether or not he was the man from the bathroom. "It was nice meeting you, *Zoey*. And—"

"Detective Grayson Rivers," Grayson offered with a tip of his head.

Ron's face paled when he cleared his throat. "If you'll excuse me, I hear my cell phone ringing in my office."

"I'll call later for that appointment," I told Glori before whisking Grayson out the door. Trembling, I parted ways with him and made a beeline for the passenger's side of his Bronco parked out front.

Without looking in my direction, Grayson slipped

his sunglasses on before starting the vehicle and pulling into the road. As the wind whipped through my unruly locks, I closed my eyes and inhaled the fresh ocean air. While meeting the Finkles wasn't necessarily a brush with death, I had never been so grateful to be alive.

"Can't wait to hear what that was about," Grayson said after a few blocks.

I dropped my head back on the headrest and turned to him. "How'd you know where to find me?"

"I was on my way to the station and spotted you through the window." He chuckled softly. "With all that red hair, you're kinda hard to miss."

"Before we go to the station, we need to find a quiet place to talk. There's something I have to tell you."

Glancing my way, his lips quirked with a sly grin. "I'm guessing by the way you kissed me back there, it has something to do with Island Sunshine Rentals."

I ducked my chin to hide the heat spreading across my neck. "I'm so sorry I put you in that situation. I should've come up with a better lie. I panicked."

"Apology accepted." He nudged my arm with his elbow. "Just don't let it happen again."

WHEN GRAYSON CONTINUED to pace the shoreline over and over for minutes on end, elbows pointed at the sky as he gripped the back of his neck and stomped barefooted through the sand, I exchanged urgent texts with Molly.

SOS! SOS! I told Grayson about the note Smith found and the fact that I think the attack in the bathroom came from the same person. He's not taking it so well.

Three dots flashed briefly before Molly's reply whooshed onto my phone's screen.

Ummm…why would u think those 2 things were related?

I was quick to tap out a fast reply.

Because the man in the bathroom said something about stopping my search for Ginny b4 Lucky attacked him. And Grayson saved me from an encounter with the man who is most likely behind it all.

The telltale dots of Molly's response appeared.

Then went away. Then reappeared. I huffed as the cycle continued without any actual response.

As Grayson marched back toward me, his expression stoic, I sent one last message to my bestie.

PLZ don't freak. I need u on my side.

I tossed my phone between my legs in the sand and blocked the intense sunlight spilling over Grayson's shoulder as he approached. My pulse raced when he plopped down into the sand at my side and draped his arms over his bent knees.

"You remind me of my last girlfriend," he began, eyes fixed on the waves rolling in. "Bexley was brave, and smart. A bit stubborn. Often ready with a smart comeback." His mouth crooked with a slight smile. "Easy on the eyes."

So far, his reaction wasn't as bad as I had been expecting. "Easy on the eyes" was lightyears better than the usual "cute" or "adorable", and he was comparing me to the not-so-horrifying ex. Stomach fluttering, I mirrored his pose, bumping my elbow against his. "Let me guess. You broke up with her because she kept important secrets from you?"

"No." He shifted his sunglasses to the top of his head and turned to me, squinting against the harsh rays of the mid-morning light. "We didn't make it as a couple because she was always placing herself in dangerous situations. I couldn't tell you how many times she almost got killed in her quest to become a private investigator."

"I'm sorry if I've stirred up bad memories." All at once I understood why he'd been so protective when learning I worked late and walked home alone, and his persistence on my being able to defend myself. "I only want justice for whoever's remains I found in that parking lot. I promise you I don't have any aspirations to be a private investigator."

"But you and Bexley share a natural curiosity that drives you to make reckless decisions." His features hardened. "You didn't know what you were walking into back there, Zoey. If Ron Finkle is the one sending you threats, those threats could escalate with time. Especially now that he knows you've made him as your potential stalker. If he did something to Ginny, he'll be desperate to keep the truth buried."

"I know that now. Believe me, I learned my lesson by going there alone. I won't do it again. I'm not as brave as you think." I set my hand on his shoulder. "I'm sorry, Grayson. I wish I would've told you everything right away instead of making the stupid decision to confront Ron."

"Me too." He held my gaze for a moment, jaw flexing, before he turned back to face the Gulf. "Wanna know what I hate most about all of this?"

Afraid I'd upset him even more with the wrong answer, I remained quiet.

"I enjoyed the hell outta that kiss," he confessed.

A sharp breath passed over my lips. The disclosure was most unexpected as I was sure the kiss had irritated him. Maybe even to the point of being revolted. "Does that mean you no longer see me as someone's kid sister?"

He huffed with a short laugh. "I told myself that needed to be my role with you. I thought you were too young and, at times, a little naive. I figured it was the safest way to prevent something from developing between us. But I was into you from the start, and I've learned over time you're not so green behind the ears. I decided you were just...*nervous* around me. Truth is, I've been wanting to kiss you for days."

"Wow. I did *not* see any of this coming. I mean you're spot on about the talking thing—must be those detective skills at play. But everything else..." I waited for his gaze to meet mine, hopeful it meant he would kiss me again, but he wouldn't look away from the water. "Why haven't you made a move?"

"Because I'm not ready to jump back into a relationship—especially now that I know you're a lot like Bexley. I won't stand by a second time to watch someone I care about repeatedly put themselves in harm's way, no matter how hard I beg them to stop." He squeezed my knee and finally turned back to me with a slack expression. "And you're not the kind of person I could have a mere fling with, then walk away from once it was over."

His words and the disappointment in his alluring eyes made me want to kiss him again. I *really* liked him, and I wished our relationship had taken a different turn. But it sounded as if his experience with his last girlfriend had really done him in, and I only knew a tiny fraction of what he had been through. What could I possibly say to change his mind?

Tears stung behind my eyelids when I nodded. "I shouldn't have pushed you that way. Like I said, I wasn't thinking at the time. I was just incredibly relieved to see you." I nudged him with my knee. "You can be awfully somber at times, but I have a lot of fun with you. You make me laugh. And not many people take me so seriously. I wouldn't have *dreamed* of kissing you if I knew it'd cost our friendship."

"Zoey, I'm still your friend. What happened won't stop me from helping you find Ginny. But I'm going to need you to think carefully before you do anything that might put your life in danger." He clambered to his feet and extended his hand. One of his cute smiles finally brought light back into his lovely brown eyes. "Let's go tell the chief everything you just told me. I have a feeling he'll want to bring Ron in for questioning."

TWELVE

Hours later, as I waited alone in Grayson's truck outside the police station, I nibbled on my already chipped finger- nails. I had made colossal mistakes in my quest to find Ginny, and would give anything to take them back. Now I was forced to face the consequences of my mistakes—one that involved Ron Finkle being interviewed without me present.

I'd made an even bigger mistake in angering the dark-haired detective emerging from the police station. My fantasy of licking his tattooed skin had evaporated right before my very eyes, all because of my deceptive ways. The idea that I could've possibly had him if I had been honest made my stomach dip and swell.

"Well?" I demanded, springing out of the truck. "What did he say? Did he admit to harassing me?"

Grayson slipped his sunglasses back over his eyes. "Get back in the vehicle. I promised the chief we'd be long gone by the time he releases Ron Finkle."

Mouth agape, my eyes bulged. "He's *releasing* him? Did the chief look at his injury underneath the gauze? Ron looked rattled when he found me standing in his building, Grayson! I know it was him!"

"Get in, Zoey," he repeated with a bite to his words. "I'll explain everything on our way to pick up Lucky."

Forcing a sharp breath, I complied. We were a block away when he glanced in my direction. "Ron's injuries were inconclusive. They could've been from a dog's teeth, or they could've been from a nail in a fence as he claimed. And he has a credible alibi—he was playing poker with a group of friends. The chief is going to check up on it."

My hands fisted in my lap. "Did he ask Ron about that sports car parked outside the rental agency?"

"It's Ron's," he confirmed. At the stop sign, he turned to me. "But you told the chief you didn't know a make, model, or color of the car you saw parked outside my house."

I scolded myself for not paying better attention to Todd the Terrible's obsession with different makes of sports cars. "Did he check to see if Ron had sent a message to my number?"

"He did. Ron was more than willing to hand his phone over for inspection. The chief was unable to find any incriminating message."

"He could've deleted it."

"All these things could be coincidental, Zoey." He shook his head while turning a corner. "Ron's injury, a dark colored sports car, even the pen. You said it yourself that the pen could've been picked up by anyone."

"Did he admit to knowing Ginny?"

"No. The chief blindsided him with her name in the middle of questioning. Ron seemed genuinely unaffected."

"Could the chief give him a lie detector test?"

"We don't have enough probable cause." Grayson veered into the animal hospital's parking lot. "I'm not convinced Ron is the one threatening you."

"Who else could it be?"

"I don't know." He killed the engine and twisted in his seat, resting his hand behind my head. "But there's some good news to come out of this. Ginny has made her way onto Chief Shaw's radar. Because of your statement, he opened an active case involving the threats you've been given regarding her." His lips curved with a deep grin. "He's going to launch an official search for Ginny."

WE ORDERED Polly's Pizza for dinner and dined on Grayson's patio overlooking the tranquil gulf while Lucky begged for scraps. Neither of us had the heart to say no to the dog's massive brown eyes, sparkling with adoration for his new owners. We were both overwhelmed with relief when the vet informed us that Lucky was in the clear, and only needed to take it easy so as not to disturb any more stitches.

The splendor of the Florida sunset exploded across the sky in brilliant hues of pink and gold, and the clear light bulbs strung above our heads flickered to life. It was far too romantic of a setting for a couple of friends. *What a waste of a good view,* I huffed to myself.

"What happens now?" I asked while licking marinara sauce from my fingers.

"You shouldn't be alone." Grayson tossed a piece

of pepperoni at Lucky. "I think it's best if you stay here until we know more about Ginny and your stalker."

Remembering the uncomfortable sensations that came with sleeping in his bed and the morning after, I shifted in the chair. "I'm sure Molly will be around. She has the weekend off, too."

He gave me a pointed look. "I thought you said she had an active social life."

"She does. If she goes out, I'll lock the door and keep the stun gun you gave me within reach." Grayson didn't look convinced, so I added, "Annnnnd I promise not to do anything stupid that would not meet your approval."

"It's still a better idea to stay here with me. If it really was Ron sending those—"

"I don't want to stay here," I blurted, holding the palms of my hands up between us. "I'm sorry, but it was super awkward sleeping in your bed. Between your scent being everywhere, including on your shirt...it was a little overwhelming." Heat rushed into my cheeks. "Especially now that I know...you know...those things you said...about wanting to kiss me...etcetera."

He appeared to be indifferent with my confession, dark gaze locked with mine, lips pressed tightly together. *Change your mind about me,* I silently pleaded with a look. For a heart-stopping moment, it seemed as if he was ready to give in. His eyes softened, and his lips parted. Perhaps for a kiss or a revelation. Then the spell broke with the buzzing of his cell phone on the glass table next to the pizza box.

"I'll be right back," he said dismissively, plucking his phone off the table and slipping inside the house.

Lucky whined and set his chin on my lap. I scratched behind his ear, watching seagulls play along the shore as the sun sunk behind the horizon. "I know, buddy. I feel the exact same way."

My own phone began to buzz in my pocket.

I answered to hear Molly say, "What's happenin', hot stuff?"

"I'm still at Grayson's. It's been a crazy day, but at least we were able to bring Lucky home."

"How is our little fighter?"

I scratched behind his ear, giggling when he thumped a hind leg against the stone. "He's back to his old self."

"And your hottie detective?"

"He's *not mine,*" I clarified, glancing over my shoulder to ensure Grayson was still inside. "This afternoon he made it clear that nothing will ever happen between us. I need to get outta here."

"Then my timing couldn't be more on point. Get your cute little butt back to our place. We're getting dressed up and goin' out to show off your dance moves with Beckett—and Teenie! Smith said Stormbringer is on their way to play at the bar. I guess they had a cancelation somewhere else after they were all geared up to go."

"Hallelujah!" Stormbringer was a legendary 80s cover band from the area that drew in massive crowds. "I'll be there in ten!"

I ended the call and kissed the dog on his head. "Momma's goin' out!" Lucky barked happily. I grabbed the half-empty pizza box and gathered the rest of our garbage, then crept back inside with the dog on my heels. Grayson was still on the phone, listening intently to whoever was on the other end of the call.

As I finished tidying up, Grayson held up one hand, motioning for me to wait. "I appreciate the call, Ginger. This information could prove to be valuable. Yep…right…okay. I'll be in touch."

Excitement sparked my belly as he slipped his phone into his pocket. "Was that Ginny's sister?"

"It was," he confirmed. "She verified that Anton Wells, Elizabeth Wells's father and Ginny's maternal grandfather, lived in Destin before he passed from heart failure. Ginny was his only grandchild. They remained close even though all ties had been severed between Ginny and Elizabeth. The grandfather insisted they keep their meetings a secret so as not to upset his daughter. Ginger said Ginny was always convinced she'd inherit everything from her grandfather, including the house." A tired look passed over his expression as he ran a hand through his hair. "Once Ginger heard Anton had died, she hired a private investigator to look into the status of his estate. She learned everything he owned had, in fact, been left to Ginny. Elizabeth had contested the will and lost. Everything was auctioned off within two months of Anton's death for over thirty mil. No one has been able to find Ginny since. The PI told Ginger all of her bank accounts had been emptied."

I whistled. "That's a fat stack. It would've made it easy for Ginny to disappear. I'll bet Elizabeth was piiiised. Where's mommy dearest now?"

"The PI located her on a manifesto for a flight headed to one of the Philippine Islands around the time of the estate sale, but her trail went cold from there."

"Did you get the address of the grandfather's property?"

"Ginger didn't remember the *exact* address, but

she was able to tell me the street and the general area. She said she had only been there once in college to drop Ginny off."

"Did Ginger say who owns the property now?"

"She didn't know, but we could find out through public tax records. I'll make a few calls on Monday."

In other words, it was another dead end. At least for the time being.

"Let me know what you find out," I said, slinging my handbag over my head. I glanced at the dog, already curled in his kennel outside of Grayson's room, sound asleep. "Don't forget to keep an eye on his wound, and give him his pills in the morning."

When I took a step toward the front door, Grayson stepped in my way. "Where are you going?"

"To hang out with my friends." My heart sped with the close proximity of his lips to mine. I took a step back and folded my arms. "Not that I need your permission, *Dad*, but we're going dancing. Can you deal with it?"

"Do you really think that's a good idea?" When I narrowed my eyes with defiance, he dropped his head back with a quiet groan. "Come on, Zo. I have every reason to be worried about you."

"If you're really that worried, then I guess you'll have to come dancing with us. And I mean you have to get on the dance floor, and move your feet to the music."

His eyebrows shot upward. "Seriously?"

"Those are the conditions." With an exaggerated shrug, I stepped around him and continued my exit.

"Where?" he called after her.

"Beach Bummers." I waved a hand over my head as I reached for the door handle.

"Fine!" He quickly moved in behind me, nudging me aside to open the door. I heard the jingle of keys in his other hand. "But I'm giving you a ride."

Following him back to the truck, I felt a zing of satisfaction. Just because he wasn't ready for a relationship with me didn't mean I couldn't show off my dancing skills and give him a taste of what he was missing.

THIRTEEN

After several hours of dancing barefoot in the sand at Beach Bummers, exhaustion made its way down to my bones. The band had played half an hour after the island's midnight noise curfew as over half of the locals were in attendance. Because several of the band members were old friends with Smith, they'd invited him to join them on stage to sing a few songs.

Grayson danced along with our gang a handful of times, once during a slow song with Teenie. He impressed every last one of us with his genuine attempt to keep up. He'd gone well beyond the standard middle-aged man's moves of grinding against a partner, or pumping their fists in the air while gyrating their hips. He'd even dipped and twirled me around a few times with impeccable timing. I felt a spark of jealousy when I realized one of his exes had probably taught him those moves.

Once the band began to pack their instruments, Beckett, Molly, Grayson, and I claimed stools at the bar. Grayson had escorted Teenie home an hour prior on the Gorilla Bus. Although many of the patrons left immediately after the band's last song, my friends and I typically stayed until well after last call. A few times we had even stayed long enough to watch the sunrise.

As Grayson guzzled a glass of water, I shamelessly watched his tattoo stretch over his broad forearm. I couldn't help but notice the way his soft black button-down, short-sleeved with a tan bamboo print, accentuated his smooth pectoral muscles when he'd danced.

"They were awesome," he declared, setting his empty glass on the bar top. "I haven't danced like that in years."

With a glossy-eyed grin, Beckett glanced up from his fresh blueberry mule. "Better take it easy on the H2O, Sinatra. Wouldn't want you getting too crazy."

The fact that Grayson had stuck to water all night sent a ripple of irritation through me. I knew from experience he wasn't a teetotaler. "He's abstaining because he thinks he has to babysit me. He doesn't see me as an intelligent, capable woman with a college degree." I waved a finger in front of me. "Oh no. He sees me as a curious little monkey that makes horrible decisions. He thinks it'll one day get me murdered like that poor lady I found by the dumpster. But you guys wanna know what *I* think?" With a half-drunken, half-bitter snort, I held my margarita up in the air. *"Carpe diem, bitches!"*

Beckett and Molly exchanged an earnest look before they cheered half-heartedly, clinking their glasses with mine. A few other patrons sitting at the tiki bar hollered along, most likely clueless to the content of our conversation.

Scowling, Grayson wrapped his fingers around my forearm. "Zoey," he whispered with a heavy sigh. "That's not fair."

I jerked away from him. "Yo, Finnster!" I called, slapping my hand on the bar. "How about a round of tequila shots for your favorite coworkers?"

"I think it's time to call it a night," Grayson interjected, waving a hand to stop Finn as he approached from the service side of the bar.

"Are you giving me a curfew, *grandpa*?" I snorted in an unfeminine-like laugh.

Balking, Finn pointed at Grayson. "Wait. This guy's your grandpa?"

I spun on my stool to face Finn. "You didn't know? He's—"

My butt continued to slide all the way off of the stool. I landed so hard in the sand that I was shocked I didn't bite my tongue clean off. "Ow."

While my friends erupted in laughter, Grayson was quick to loop an arm around my waist and lift me back onto my feet. "Party's over," he declared, keeping his arm locked around my waist. "Either you're coming to my place, or Molly is going home with you."

Beside us, Molly wolfed down the last of her drink and swiped her wristlet from the bar. "Hold up! I'm coming!"

After wishing the others a good night, Grayson began to lead me away from the bar. As the clamor of the others faded behind us, he said, "You couldn't be more wrong about my perception of you. I'm only protective because I couldn't deal if you somehow got hurt."

With a rush of guilt, I leaned against him.

ON THE STREET in front of our house, Grayson let the truck idle. "I'm glad you forced me to tag along. I can't remember the last time I had that much fun."

"Probably when the doctor slapped your bare behind and announced you were a boy," I retorted with a snicker.

"Okay!" Molly reached for the door handle. "On that incredibly snarky note, I believe I'll slip inside and give you two a minute to work things out."

"No need." Looping my arm through hers, I lifted my chin defiantly in Grayson's direction. "There isn't anything for us to work out."

"You're wrong about that," he disagreed, resting his forearm on the steering wheel. "But we'll talk tomorrow." Grimacing, he eyed the stone path among palm trees leading up to Teenie's baby blue bungalow. "At least let me walk you to the door."

"No need for that either," I told him, sliding off the bench seat behind Molly.

"If you need me—"

"Better hurry home and let Lucky out." I slammed the door shut and threw him a curt wave. "Good night, Detective Rivers."

One corner of his mouth twitched in a failed effort to smile. "Good night, ladies."

The truck inched forward and disappeared into the darkness.

Molly waited for me at the bottom of the bungalow's front step, arms folded and one foot tapping. "You were super harsh on him, Zo."

"You weren't there when he said he liked me and wanted to kiss me, but I was too immature and nothing would happen between us because I'm too much like his ex." I nudged past her, digging my house keys from my pocket. "It was humiliating."

"Give him time to get to know you better. No matter what he says, I can tell he's super into you. He won't be able to keep resisting you after the moves you showed him tonight. You two totally looked like a couple when you danced!"

Sighing, my shoulders bowed forward. "But what if I really *am* just like his last girlfriend? I have no desire to put myself in another life-threatening situation like this morning when I was going to confront that *Ron* dude. Seriously, Mol, it was the worst. I was sure him and his wife were gonna chop me up and feed me to their gang of monster koi fish."

"I beg your pardon?" a deep voice boomed from somewhere within the nearby bushes.

Molly and I yelped, flinging our arms around each other.

"Who's there?" I cried, wishing I had relieved myself before we'd left the bar.

On our other side, Grayson materialized with his gun aimed at the bushes. "Come out of there with your hands up!" he ordered in a deeper than usual baritone. If I hadn't been so terrified, I may have found his "detective mode" extremely sexy.

A man arose from the bushes and dropped something at his feet. It made a metallic clang. Molly and I, still attached at the hip, scurried in the opposite direction as the man crept out from the bushes, hands lifted toward the black sky. He was just far enough from the front step's lights that his face remained concealed by shadows.

"Who are you?" Grayson demanded.

"Wait!" Molly let go of me to grab her cell phone from her wristlet. She activated the flashlight and shined it directly into the man's face.

Ron Finkle flinched, jerking his head away from the light. "Turn that off!" Dressed in black jogger pants and a black moisture-wicking shirt, he definitely wasn't out showing houses to potential renters.

"I knew it!" I shouted, pumping a fist in the air. "It *was* you harassing me all this time! You and Glori totally wanted to chop me up earlier today and feed me to your fish!"

Molly's wide eyes volleyed between me and Ron. "Who would do that?"

"My sweet Glori and I would never!" Ron barked in reply. "Violence makes us both squeamish!"

Grayson kept his gun pointed at Ron. "Are you carrying any weapons?"

"Of course not!" Ron barked in an offended tone. "What do you people think this is? I'm not a *thug!*"

"Only *thugs* dress like that and sneak around people's yards this late at night," Molly informed him. She lifted her hands out at her sides. "Just saying."

"Well I'm not one!" Ron sniffed.

Grayson tilted his head toward the bushes. "What did you drop over there?"

"It was only a can of spray paint. I was going to write Zoey a strongly-worded message, demanding she leave Ginny alone!"

"Depending on your choice of strong words, you could've been charged with a terroristic threat." In a few long strides, Grayson rushed in to pat Ron down from head to toe before returning his gun to his waistband. "What's your connection to Ginny?"

Ron slowly lowered his arms. "We were in love.

We'd been having an affair for years. I was going to leave my wife for her."

He must not have been aware of Ginny's other lovers, I decided with a humph. Eyes narrowed, I brought my fists to my hips. "But then your 'sweet Glori' found out about the affair, and demanded you kill Ginny?"

"What? No!" Ron spat, teeth bared. "Leave my wife out of this!"

Molly hummed. "Ginny decided she was only with you because she had daddy issues, so you killed her?"

Ron squeezed his eyes shut and rapidly shook his head. "I didn't kill anyone, damn it!"

Grayson passed us a sharp look. "How about we let him tell his story without any more interruptions?" He pointed at Ron. "I hope you're aware it would be pointless for you to run at this point."

Cocking his head, Ron smoothed his mustache with a trembling hand. "Am I under arrest?"

Ignoring the question, Grayson gestured to the bungalow's front step. "Have a seat, Mr. Finkle."

Ron let out a long, shuddering breath and plopped down near me. I leaped away from him, grabbing Molly again before I fell.

In a squared stance directly in front of Ron,

Grayson crossed his arms over his chest. "When did you last see Ginny?"

"I don't remember the exact date." Ron hunched forward, fingers repeatedly smoothing the creases on his tanned forehead. "All I know is it was the last time she worked at Beach Bummers."

Grayson glanced my way, eyebrows lifted.

"We had made plans to run away together the following week," Ron continued, "but I was going to surprise her at the end of her shift that night with an engagement ring. I wanted to ask her to marry me on the beach under the full moon."

"Aww," Molly cooed, clasping her hands together. "That's *super* romantic!"

I leaned in closer to my friend. "He was married to Glori at the time."

Molly threw a hand over her mouth. "Oh. Right."

Throwing a sideways glance in our direction, Grayson cleared his throat. "What happened that night, Mr. Finkle?"

"I never got the chance to pop the question." Ron's brows lowered. "When I arrived at the bar, I found her in the parking lot in the midst of an argument with another woman. It was plenty heated."

Goosebumps spread over my arms.

"Did you recognize the other woman?" Grayson pressed.

"It was dark, so I didn't get a very good look at her. She didn't seem familiar."

"Do you remember what the argument was about?"

"Never did catch what they were saying." Ron shook his head over and over. "I called out to Ginny, afraid the woman was going to strike her. I must've startled the other woman. She spun around and tripped, falling face first into a cinder block. That poor woman's face had been smashed to smithereens."

"Oh!" Molly and I chorused, flinching in perfect unison.

Grayson's jaw flexed. "You didn't call nine-one-one?"

"There was no point," Ron insisted, his voice wavering. "She wasn't walking away from that fall. Besides, it was an accident! We were both afraid the police wouldn't believe Ginny hadn't done anything malicious to that woman! She was far too beautiful for prison, and I had dished out thousands for her boob job!" He set his face inside his hands and began to cry. "I had to protect my investments!"

No wonder why so many people who knew Ginny had remarked on the size of her chest, I thought.

With a hand on Ron's shoulder, Grayson softened his tone. "Ron, what did you and Ginny do after you realized the woman was dead?"

"I sent Ginny away, and told her never to return."

"Did she say how she knew the woman?"

"I didn't think to ask. Probably because I was in shock. We *both* were."

Grayson nodded. "Did you look to see if she was carrying any form of identification?"

"I didn't think of it at the time."

"What about the body?" Grayson asked.

Ron lowered his head. "I told Ginny I'd take care of it."

"And did you?"

"I dug a...*grave*...behind a rental...a block away from the bar." Ron's cries escalated into heaving sobs. "I'm so sorry! I wasn't thinking straight!"

Grayson reached for Ron's bicep, pulling him to his feet. With his other hand, he produced a pair of handcuffs. "Ron Finkle, you're under arrest for unlawful disposal of a corpse, and accessory after the fact. You have the right to remain silent..."

FOURTEEN

After Ron Finkle's arrest, I tossed and turned until the first light of dawn crept through my window. During the small bursts of time in which I had slept, my nightmares were riddled with the grotesque image of a faceless woman. As soon as I heard noises coming from the kitchen, I threw on the sky blue kimono robe my mom had gifted me on my last birthday, and padded out of my room.

Donning her peacock print robe, dark hair in a messy bun on the top of her head, Molly sat hunched over the kitchen island. With her chin resting on her knee, she watched a pot of coffee brewing. She turned to me, revealing slight shadows beneath her light blue eyes. "Hey, Zo. Did *you* get any sleep?"

"A little," I said, shivering with the memory of my nightmares. "I wish I would've just stayed up all night."

Molly huffed a laugh. "Same." She lifted her chin off of her knee. "Have you heard anything more from Grayson?"

"He sent me a text around four, letting me know they'd booked Ron, and he was heading home as soon as he finished writing his report." With a sudden yawn, I ran a hand through my crazy hair. "It's a good thing neither of us work today. Smith would've been forced to tie on an apron while we napped in the sand."

Knuckles rapped against the front door.

Molly popped off the stool and headed over to answer it. "Guessing that's Beckett. I filled him in on what happened last night, and he freaked."

With a zombie-like gait, I moved over to the island to pluck a Granny Smith from the basket on the island. "I hope you didn't tell him *everything*, considering it's an ongoing investigation." Eyes closed, I took a lazy bite and began to chomp on the sweet fruit. There wasn't enough coffee on the entire island to prevent me from falling asleep on my feet.

"Mornin'!" Grayson's deep timber exclaimed.

Eyelids springing open, I coughed up a piece of

apple as Grayson stepped inside. Hair slightly damp and neatly combed, he wore dark jean shorts with a gray t-shirt featuring Nirvana's *In Utero* cover and leather sandals. In my state of exhaustion, the only thought I could muster was: *yummy*.

Eyes lit with a twinkle of mischief, he held one of Dee Dee's signature pink boxes out while flashing me an easygoing smile. "I figured you two would be hungry this morning."

His dark gaze flashed down to my robe, then danced over my hair before his eyes locked with mine. I hadn't bothered looking in a mirror after I crawled out of bed. He probably was trying to decide if I had spent the night trapped inside a wind tunnel with a pack of feral cats.

The apple dropped from my hand, thudding against the hardwood floor.

Molly rushed forward to take the box. "How thoughtful! Zoey's *obsessed* with Dee Dee's."

"I'll be right back!" I announced, dashing back to my room. I slammed the door shut and leaned back against it, face hotter than lava. The only way I could've been more embarrassed was if he had caught me naked.

I ran into my bathroom, moaning when my reflection confirmed my worst fears. *Fresh road kill was more attractive.* I feverishly washed my face and brushed my teeth before wrangling my hair into a ponytail and throwing on a light application of makeup. I fell over while wrangling on a fresh pair of underwear, and got my arm stuck over my head when whipping on a clean t-shirt. By the time I made it back out into the kitchen, panting under my breath, Grayson and Molly were down to the last few bites of their donuts.

"I was beginning to think you had climbed out a window and hitched a ride to Mexico," Molly teased, wiggling her eyebrows.

Subtly flashing my tongue at my roommate, I reached inside the pink box. My heart melted a little when among the array of baked goodness, I spotted two of my favorite Bavarian cream donuts with pink frosting and white sprinkles. I peered upward, meeting Grayson's knowing grin.

"You're perfect," I blurted.

With Grayson's wide-eyed expression, Molly dissolved into a fit of belly laughter.

Realizing my mistake, my cheeks flamed. "I meant they're perfect! The donuts! The donuts are perfect! I mean—you're great too!" I spread my hands over my face. "Oh my god. I'm so damn tired," I muttered.

A deep laugh rumbled in Grayson's chest. "You've had an eventful couple of days." He tugged on one of my elbows, moving my hand away from my face, and patted the open stool between us. "Sit and eat your donuts while I walk you through the next steps."

I snagged one of the donuts, smacking my giggling roommate on the back before I settled next to Grayson. Still mortified by my faux pas, I stared down on the donut in my hand while he spoke.

"The chief called Avery this morning to see if she could fill out Ginny's warrant for a judge to sign," he told us. "But she spent a good part of the weekend in the hospital with stomach pains, so they're running tests to find out what's going on. It's going to slow things up since the chief and I aren't too familiar with the computer system. There's no rush anyway since I doubt the warrant will get us anywhere. The last known address we could find for Ginny was here on the island. Beyond that, we couldn't find a trace of her existence. No vehicle registered in her name, no property, no court records of any kind. It's almost like she vanished."

"Just like her birth mom," I realized, straightening my back before turning to him. "Maybe she hitched a ride with her to the Philippine Islands."

"It's a possibility," Grayson agreed with a slight nod.

"*Orrrr*," Molly trilled, one frosted-finger held up, "maybe Ginny had a secret evil twin, and Ron accidentally killed Ginny instead of the sister, so he created the story about *another* woman because he feels massive regret for killing the woman he loved."

I momentarily stopped chewing and stared at her. "We *really* need to wean you off Teenie's soap operas."

Grayson reached over me, taking one of the chocolate eclairs. "We're hoping to schedule an excavation of the woman's remains once the prosecutor has had a chance to work out a deal with Ron Finkle's attorney in exchange for showing us where he buried her."

"That poor woman." I shivered when recalling the details Ron had provided. "Will they be able to identify her once they've recovered the rest of her body?"

Swaying his head back and forth, he licked the frosting from his fingers. "It will depend on the level of decay, and whether or not she was buried with anything that might help speed up the process. Normally it can take weeks or months." He took a bite of the eclair and shrugged while chewing the pastry on one side of his mouth. "Without a skull to go by dental work, I'm not convinced it's entirely possible. We'll know more once the remains are in the hands of a forensic pathologist."

We sat in comfortable silence for a handful of moments, scarfing down our donuts. The rush of sugar slowly began to clear the tequila fog from my brain. "Do you think Ron was lying when he claimed he didn't know who she was?" I asked.

"Maybe," he answered with another mouthful. "The prosecutor is considering dropping all charges if Ron shows us where she was buried and gives us a name."

Molly bit into a donut, spraying bits of its jelly filling when she spoke. "I still don't think you should rule out an evil twin."

I shot her an annoyed look before glancing back Grayson's way. "If you don't have a way to identify her, couldn't he just give you a bogus name to keep himself out of jail?"

He shook his head. "We would have to somehow verify the name he provided was legitimate before the charges would be dropped."

"We need to contact the private investigator Ginger hired," I decided. "Maybe he could tell us more about the estate sale, and give us the address to the grandfather's house. We could talk to the neighbors and whoever bought the place. Maybe—"

Grayson's elbow brushed over my ribcage. "I appreciate your enthusiasm, Zoey, and that's not a bad idea, but this is now an official police investigation. If you start poking around into Ginny's past, you could accidentally impede the process and somehow tip Ginny off that we're searching for her."

The momentum whooshed from my excitement. "You mean I can't do *anything* to help find Ginny from this point on? You wouldn't have caught Ron and discovered this woman if I hadn't insisted on searching for her even though the chief thought it was a waste of time."

"I know, and your dedication won't go unnoticed." He knocked his bare knee against mine. "For now, I'll keep you up-to-date as best as I can. If I can think of any other way to get you involved without crossing a line, I'll let you know."

GRAYSON RETURNED to the station shortly after finishing his last donut. Molly went back to bed, and Teenie returned from beach yoga to camp out in front of the television. Unable to sit still for longer than five minutes at a time, I slipped into my tennis shoes and took off without a destination in mind.

I ended up jogging all the way to Grayson's house to tend to Lucky. I sat on the patio with him for a while, feeding him cold pizza to hold his attention as I vented.

"Maybe telling your new daddy I'd found a skull wasn't the best idea after all," I told my new buddy, tossing him a bite-sized chunk. "I could've made it this far without his help. Then again, maybe Ron and Glori really would've fed me to their koi fish if your daddy hadn't been there, and who knows what Ron would've done to us last night if your daddy hadn't been there that time too. But still." Lucky wolfed the pizza down in a matter of seconds, and begged for more. Rolling my eyes, I fed him another chunk. "What am I doing? I must be way beyond exhausted if I expect you to comprehend anything I'm saying."

Lucky finished chewing and barked.

"I know," I told him, scratching the fur beneath his cone.

Since Grayson didn't think he'd be back until late and Lucky was on strict orders not to move around too much, I called the Gorilla Bus. Lucky and I rode around the island for hours. I chatted with every group of passengers to ride during that time, catching up with other locals who didn't see the need for their own vehicle, and losing myself in the tourists' stories.

Whenever the bus was empty, I got to know Driver Stewy a little better. The skinny 20-year-old with blond dreadlocks was saving up to move out of his parents' basement and buy a steel drum set so he could join a reggae band and travel the world. He had painted the neon graffiti-like illustrations covering the roof of the eccentric bus after a computer engineer from Silicon Valley had given him a batch of psychedelic mushrooms. Some of them were quite good, and some looked as if they had been drawn by a kid high on mushrooms.

Lucky was content resting his pillow cone on the edge of the window ledge and inhaling every scent the island had to offer. Whenever he whined to be let out, Stewy lovingly carried him up and down the steps.

Late in the afternoon, while Stewy was busy hitting on a group of sixteen-year-olds from Chicago, I laid back in one of the seats and closed my eyes. *Just for a minute or two,* I told myself.

Before I knew it, I awoke to darkness at the shrill sound of Lucky's urgent barks. The bus was once again empty.

"I wasn't sure if you wanted me to wake you," Stewy called from the driver's seat. "You were, like, super out of it. At one point I thought maybe you needed an exorcism the way you were making noises and thrashing around."

My cheeks warmed. I must've been out cold, caught up in more nightmares of the faceless woman. I bolted upright, rubbing the haze from my eyes while trying to focus on Lucky. With his one front paw on the windowsill, his gaze honed on something outside. "What's he barking at?" I asked Stewy.

"Dunno. He just started flippin' out, man. Maybe the dude has to tinkle. I haven't stopped to let him out since you fell asleep." Stewy met my gaze in the rearview mirror. "Want me to pull over?"

"Yeah, go ahead and let him out at the end of the block." I grabbed my phone from the seat beside me to check the time. In the three hours in which I'd slept, I had missed dozens of calls from Grayson, Molly, and Beckett. I quickly hit redial on Grayson's number. The call went straight to his voicemail.

I tucked my phone back inside my pocket and headed toward the front of the bus. The second Stewy opened the door, Lucky darted down the steps before either of us had a chance to hold him back. He sprinted away on his three limbs as if he wasn't missing the fourth. It was equal parts impressive and frightening.

I tossed a $20 bill at Stewy. "Sorry, it's all I have on me! I'll give you more next time I see you!"

"No worries, Zoey!" Stewy called to my back as I ran after Lucky. "Give me a holler if you ever need a doggy sitter!"

I stopped short when my eyes adjusted to the street lights. I hadn't been paying attention when I woke, and didn't realize Stewy had dropped me a block away from Beach Bummers. Construction vehicles beeped and roared from somewhere nearby. It wasn't totally unheard of for them to work after dark, but the only instance I remembered was after the island's main waterline had burst.

"Lucky!" I called out while attempting to call Grayson again. "Here boy!"

Worry cramped my stomach. If I didn't find Lucky soon, he might tear another stitch. And what if I completely lost him? Grayson and I would both be devastated. Even though we'd only known the dog for a short while, he had nestled his way into our hearts.

With the sound of more barking off to my right— in the opposite direction of the bar—I huffed out a relieved breath and took off running in the same direction. The construction noises grew louder along with Lucky's persistent barks.

As I rounded the corner of the island's only apartment complex, a large cluster of spotlights came into view. Grayson, Chief Shaw, and Deputy Hughes conversed with the driver of an excavator, each of them wearing navy windbreakers labeled "POLICE" in reflective tape. At least a dozen of the county sheriff's deputies and a team of city workers in bright orange vests and hardhats gathered around them. In handcuffs and an orange jumpsuit, Ron Finkle pointed at different spots in a community garden beyond a patch of St. Augustine grass. An attorney I recognized as being a regular at the tiki bar stood at Ron's side.

I sucked in a sharp breath. *They were preparing to dig for the woman's body.*

Relief washed over Grayson's stone-faced expression as I crept closer to the site of the excavation. He exchanged quick words with the chief before darting over to meet me.

The way he seized my forearms and leaned in, eyes alive with something I couldn't name, I was sure he was going to kiss me. "Where the hell have you been? Why haven't you been answering your phone?"

"I'm sorry. I fell asleep on the Gorilla Bus. Have you seen Lucky?"

His head jerked back. "That was him barking?"

"Yeah. He rode around with me all afternoon. I woke when he started barking like a maniac. I thought maybe he had to pee, but he bolted outside when the driver opened the door."

Grayson's focus snapped to something over my shoulder. "There he is! Come here, boy!"

Heart swelling with joy, I spun around.

Then, it was as if someone had deflated my heart with a needle. When I spotted Lucky, I hoped maybe my tired eyes were deceiving me. Lips parted with a silent gasp, my pulse slowed to a bone-rattling thud.

Lucky had brought us a present of considerable size.

I blindly reached for Grayson, swatting his chest with urgency. "Is that—?"

"*Holy…shit,*" Grayson muttered softly.

Lucky dropped the missing skull at our feet.

FIFTEEN

I wasn't sure if we should scold Lucky for possibly damaging the skull with his teeth, or reward him with a lifetime supply of milk bones. "Do you suppose…" I started, holding a hand over my erratic heart. *Did people my age experience cardiac arrest?* I licked my parted lips and tried again. "I mean do you think…" I was too stunned to finish, and my chest had become too tight to wrench another breath.

The sudden presence of Grayson's firm hand on my back steadied my heartbeats. "He could've removed the skull the night you found it by the dumpster. He could even be the one that found the woman's burial site, and dug it up."

"What if that's why he got so excited," I wheezed, "you know, because he remembered where he'd put it?"

"Then our boy is smarter than we thought." Grayson edged me forward with a light push. "See if you can get him to come to you. You can restrain him while I snatch the skull."

On wobbly legs, I slowly squatted down to the pavement. "Come, Lucky," I rasped, pointing down by my feet. "Here, boy. Be a good boy, and *come*. Daddy wants your present."

"*Daddy*?" Grayson sniggered above me.

Lucky titled his head, whining in question. I reached out to him. "Come on, buddy."

The dog growled with a soft gurgle. It wasn't anything remotely close to the threatening way he had growled at Ron in the bathroom. Then his lips parted and his tongue flopped to the side like he was smiling. He wagged his tail and barked several times before nudging the skull with his nose.

Once I realized what was happening, I gasped. "Grayson!" I hissed from one side of my mouth. "He wants to *play catch.*"

"Pretend you're all for it," he told me in a quiet, steady voice. "Just reach down and grab the skull, then hand it to me."

"I am *not* grabbing the skull. That was someone's *head*."

"If you don't do it, he might pick it up and run off with it. He thinks it's a toy." Grayson nudged my rear with the toe of his loafer. "Hurry before he stashes it somewhere again."

"Okay, buddy," I told Lucky. "You're gonna owe me big time for this." Wincing, I lengthened my right arm as far as it would go, and waddled forward a few inches until my fingers brushed over one of the skull's eye sockets. I attempted to swallow the squeal that came from my lips, but it came out in a piercing whine. Lucky's sharp, excited barks rattled against my ear drums.

"Grab it, Zoey," Grayson urged. "Fast, like tearing off a bandaid."

"What if I can't?" I cried in earnest.

"You can."

I held Lucky's stare when he started doing the weird growl thing again. "What if I drop it?"

"You won't."

"That just proves you don't know me very well yet. I tend to drop things."

"Do it, and I'll take you out on a date."

I snapped my head around to look up at him. "What about my naivety, and my tendency to make reckless decisions?" Beneath his dark gaze, my skin tingled with electricity. "I thought you weren't ready for another relationship."

"I'm still not, so we'll have to take it extra slow. Not even a *glimpse* of first base for at least three to six months...or maybe until you turn another year older."

My entire body ignited with the idea of there being *bases* between us.

His lips split with a grin. "Better hurry and do it before the offer expires."

With a drawn-out squeal, I plunged my fingers into the depth of the eye socket and hooked them around the first crevice they came in contact with. A grotesque moment later, I was standing with the skull cradled against my stomach like a quarterback preparing to make the winning pass.

"Oh god!" I wheezed, extending my neck far away from my hands and twisting my head away. "Oh god! I'm seriously holding a *woman's head* in *my hands!*"

"Easy does it," Grayson said with a soft chuckle. As he stretched his hands out to me, Lucky let out two demanding barks. "Hand it to me."

We moved together slowly, trying not to agitate Lucky any further. Grayson's large hands slid over mine, gripping the dog's treasured gift with care. The gold tooth inside its mouth caught in one of the spotlights.

Grayson's eyes held mine. "You'll have to hold him back while I take this over to the forensic team. Ready?"

With a slight nod, I slowly withdrew my hands. I dove at Lucky, relieved when he didn't fight as I looped my arms beneath his neck pillow. As Grayson hustled back toward the site of the excavation, I anchored Lucky's stout body to the pavement with a good portion of my weight.

Lucky licked his lips and let out a high-pitched whine.

"I know, buddy," I told him. "I know. But you're a *really* good, good boy."

I smiled to myself as I buried my face in his thick fur, hoping it wouldn't be long before they'd reunite the woman's head with her body.

———

THE PROCESS of recovering the rest of the woman's remains was completed in under an hour. After one of the sheriff's K-9 deputies worked with Lucky, allowing him to sniff the skull then leading him to the garden before repeating the same steps several times, our 3-legged pet began to paw at a section of dirt. Grayson placed Lucky in the back of a police cruiser while the forensic team began to cautiously uncover dirt until they came across a clavicle.

"It's all here!" a woman from the forensic team confirmed, followed by a brief round of applause.

I watched on with a sense of peace, my eyes brimming with unshed tears.

"You did it, Zo," Grayson whispered, hugging me close to his side. "This woman can finally be at peace because of you."

Swiping my arm across my eyes, I shook my head. "Not until we find Ginny. If this really isn't her, there has to be some kind of repercussions for what they did. It wasn't right to rob this woman's family of a proper burial."

Grayson's arm dropped from around me as Chief Shaw approached, head bowed and his POLICE baseball hat wrenched between his thick fingers. "Zoey, I owe you an apology. If I had listened to you from the beginning—"

"Then it may have taken us longer to find this woman without her help," Grayson cut in.

"Or without Lucky's," I added, lifting my chin and smiling triumphantly.

The chief barked with a gruff laugh. "I just might have to offer that dog a job with the department after tonight."

"What about me?" I blurted, surprising myself.

"What?" Grayson and the chief chorused.

"Grayson said Avery has been out sick a lot with medical complications." I shuffled my feet and swallowed the lump in my throat. "I mean, I have a bachelor's degree in business, and I could really use the extra money."

"Is that right?" The chief slowly rubbed his chin. "Sounds like you might be overqualified."

"Not if we gave her more responsibilities," Grayson chimed in. "You said you've been toying with the idea of hiring another deputy to handle evidence and civil processing."

"I *am* a fast learner." I shrugged one shoulder. "I could just fill in until Avery feels better."

Chief Shaw folded his arms while regarding me with a stern expression. "You know, that might not be such a bad idea. We're going to get buried in paperwork from this case if we don't do something. Can you come in tomorrow morning?"

With an eager nod, I beamed back at him. "I

don't work at the tiki bar until four, and I'm sure I can talk Smith into finding someone to cover for me if I need to stay later."

"Then I guess we'll see how you work out." He slapped Grayson on the back. "You better get some sleep tonight, Detective. We have a long week ahead of us."

"Roger that," Grayson answered, passing me a grin.

Although the idea had come to me on a whim, I was beside myself with joy. I would no longer be forced to stand aside and do nothing in the search for Ginny.

MONDAY MORNING, I arrived half an hour earlier than Chief Shaw had requested. The station door was already unlocked, and every last light was on. I set my handbag on the top tier of the front desk and stepped around it to discover one of Dee Dee's pink boxes next to a small vase of vibrant wildflowers. A blue sticky note on top of the box read, "Good luck on your first day!" in what I recognized as Grayson's handwriting. My suspicions were confirmed when I flipped the lid open to discover two of my favorite

Bavarian cream donuts. Butterflies flooded my stomach.

"Good morning, Zoey," Chief Shaw's voice boomed.

Glancing upward, I returned his friendly smile. "Good morning, Chief."

"Hope you've had your fill of caffeine already." He stretched, rubbing his belly over his neatly pressed shirt. "With Hughes on patrol, and Grayson in Tampa to meet with forensic pathologists, I'm prepared to put a lot of responsibility on your shoulders."

Admittedly, I was a bit disappointed to learn Grayson wouldn't be in the office. I straightened my back and smoothed the skirt on the modest baby doll dress I had picked out with Grayson in mind. "I'm ready for whatever you throw my way, sir."

"Grayson told me you have a few productive ideas on ways to find Ginny Jones. Once I've completed the standard processing to make you an employee and tech has programmed you into the system, I'm going to give you free rein to do what it takes to track that woman down. If Ron Finkle is telling the truth, I want her brought in A-SAP."

I couldn't believe my good fortune. All at once, it felt as if I had discovered my dream job. "Yessir!"

The station's phone rang. I didn't hesitate to answer. "Santa Maria Island Police Department, this is Zoey. How can I help you?"

"As in Zoey, the redhead from the tiki bar?" a familiar voice asked.

"As in Zoey, the redhead from the tiki bar, moonlighting as a temporary administrator with the police department," I clarified. "Whom am I speaking with?"

"It's George Jones—Ginny's brother."

My eyes widened. "George, hi! You just happen to be on my list of calls to make. Do you know the name of that private investigator Ginger hired after Ginny's grandfather passed?"

"It was Travis something-or-other. I think he worked at Parker Investigations out of Destin. Why?"

I found a piece of scratch paper on the desk, and scribbled the information with a pen. "We have some questions for him regarding our search for Ginny."

"Does it have something to do with the human remains the police discovered last night? Do they think it's her?"

Word traveled fast, I thought. A part of me felt sorry for George and his older sister, knowing it could be a long process before anyone could confirm whether or not Ginny was still alive.

Unsure of the confidentiality rules with my new employer, I told him, "Can you please hold for a minute, George?"

Before he answered, I found the hold button and met the Chief's curious icy blues. "It's George Jones, Ginny's brother. He's inquiring about the body you found last night."

The chief's thick fingers swiped over his forehead. "Goddamn social media. The news was already all over the internet before I got out of bed this morning." Grunting, he turned away from me. "I'll take the call in my office."

I made myself comfortable behind the large laminate desk, taking a quick inventory of its drawers' orderly contents, and adjusting the height on the mesh high-back chair. I fired up the desktop computer, sniffing the flowers and taking a bite of a donut while waiting for it to load. I bypassed Avery's password by logging in as a guest, and navigated to a new tab on the internet browser. I quickly found a number for the investigator's office in Destin, and dialed it on another one of the station's phone lines.

"Parker Investigations," a woman drawled after only one ring. "Betty speaking."

"Hello, Betty." I gulped down the bite I had just taken. "This is Zoey with the Santa Maria Island Police Department. Is Travis in?"

A weighted sigh followed. "Sugar, I'm afraid Mr. Parker has passed."

I blanched. "As in died?"

"Yes, ma'am." The woman's voice lowered to a whisper. "The police think it was an accident, but Travis wasn't keen on sweets, and he certainly wouldn't have bought anything containing nuts. He was hyper-aware of his severe peanut allergy, god rest his soul. Wouldn't touch a single baked good anyone brought into the office. Wanna know what I think? Someone slipped him something with peanut dust because he got too close to their dirty secrets. Someone *wanted* him dead."

"I don't know what to say." My throat dried. "I'm…sorry for your loss."

"He was a good man," Betty said, her tone far away. She paused, then said, "Anyway, what can I do you for, sugar? Would you like to speak with one of our other investigators?"

"I was hoping someone could answer a few questions I have regarding Ginny Jones and her grandfather, Anton Wells."

"*Oh, darlin',*" Betty replied among a sharp intake

of breath. Again, her voice dropped to a whisper. "Please don't repeat this to anyone—it could cost me my job—but the day Travis died, he left for Anton Wells's estate to investigate a lead on Ginny. If you ask me, that's what got our beloved Travis killed."

SIXTEEN

"And you're certain she thought his death was related to *Ginny's* case?" Grayson asked once I had called to fill him in on the details of my conversation with the investigator's receptionist.

"Positive." Even though he couldn't see me, I nodded. "This could be big, Grayson. I can feel it in my bones."

Grayson heaved a deep sigh. "Is the chief in? I'll put in a request for us to head up to Destin as soon as I'm finished here. He has an old pilot buddy with a private jet that owes him a few favors—it'll cut down on travel time."

"Us, as in you and the chief?"

"As in me and *you*. If he approves the trip, you'll want to head home and pack an overnight bag."

Lightness passed through my chest. Grayson wanted me to travel with him in a private jet to investigate a case. I wasn't sure which part of that idea was most exciting. I checked the phone's switchboard, finding my call occupied the only active line. "He's in his office. I'll patch you through to him just as soon as I figure out how to operate this massive system."

"Your instincts for this kind of thing seem to be spot on, Zoey," Grayson said. "You're already proving you belong on our team."

I pumped a fist into the air and opened my mouth to release a silent shout of triumph, deciding maybe fate had brought me to the island so I could discover my true calling in life. "Thanks, Grayson. That means a lot coming from you." As I reached down to put him on hold, my eyes caught on the flowers. "Oh! And thank you for the flowers and donuts. That was really sweet of you. Molly's right—you're extremely thoughtful."

"Don't you mean I'm perfect?" he teased.

Warmth spread through my cheeks. "Don't push it, old man. I'm reserving judgment until after you take me on that date."

"About that…" his voice faded with uncertainty.

I winced with the sudden clench of my stomach. Had he already changed his mind, or had it only been a false offer from the start? "Grayson—"

The chief was suddenly towering above me. "That's Rivers? Tell him I'd like to have a word."

My shoulders dropped. "Chief Shaw just came out of his office and said he wants to speak with you," I told Grayson in a formal tone. "Hold on." I hit the HOLD button and tipped my chin at the chief. "He's all yours."

Hiding my budding feelings from my new boss while working alongside Grayson was going to be a challenge.

"ARE THEY GIVING YOU A BADGE?" Teenie asked, watching with rounded eyes as I feverishly packed a bag. "Or a *gun*?"

"It's not like that." I rejected another dress, discarding it into the growing pile on her floor. "I'm only going as Detective Rivers's…assistant."

"I'd be more than happy to *assist* that delicious man in whatever he needs." Teenie wiggled her drawn-in eyebrows with a cartoonish purr.

"Your little crush on him is becoming a little disconcerting, Teenie. Do me a favor and tone it down—especially if he comes inside to get me. No weird innuendoes about me and him hooking up, either. He's one of my bosses now."

Teenie hummed with a smile. "Even better. Secret office affairs add the perfect amount of spice to a relationship. It's exciting knowing at any moment the office door might open, and someone could catch you down on your—"

"Enough!" I squeezed my eyelids shut and shook my head. "I'm seriously starting to think I need to send you and Molly to rehab for your soap opera addictions!" At least Teenie had moved beyond her fear of Grayson being a murderer.

When the doorbell rang, I retrieved the last dress I'd discarded on the floor, and shoved it into my duffel bag with the rest of my things. I zipped the bag and slung it over my shoulder before shooting my landlord a narrowed look. "*Please* promise me you'll behave. I can't go on this trip with him if you're going to make things awkward."

Folding her waif arms over her stomach, Teenie's lips puckered with a pout. "Would you like me to hide in a closet?"

"The way you embarrassed me in front of him

last time? That wouldn't be the worst idea you've had." Laughing, I dropped a kiss inside her cloud of white hair. "Stay out of trouble while I'm gone. Maybe you can check in on Smith later to make sure he hasn't passed out and lost Lucky."

There was a skip in my step as I headed for the front door. Part of me wanted to launch myself into Grayson's arms when the door swung open. Only it wasn't Grayson.

Glori Finkle threw me a frazzled smile that matched the crumpled state of her pantsuit and frizzy hair. Unlike the first time we had met, Glori's ensemble didn't include a single piece of jewelry, and her face was scrubbed clean of any cosmetics. "Zoey Zastrow." Her lips quivered. "So we meet again."

Biting my bottom lip, I glanced over Glori to scan the road, wishing Grayson would come to my rescue. "Mrs. Finkle, you shouldn't be here."

"Please, call me Glori." She barged her way inside, flashing her fingers in front of her. The stench of alcohol oozed from her breath. "I no longer want anything to do with that dreadful surname."

"I'm not sure it's appropriate for us to have any kind of conversation, *Glori*. Especially when you've been day-drinking. I work for the island's Chief of Police now, and Detective Rivers is on his way here."

Glori spun around jerkily, a knowing smile growing on her lips. "You mean the sexy boyfriend?"

"He's your *boyfriend* now?" Teenie yelled from my room.

"Never mind, Teenie!" I called back. "This conversation isn't for you to hear!"

"Who was that?" Glori's sloppy gaze darted around the house. "Your mother?"

"My landlord." I shook my head. "Whatever you have to say should be conveyed in an official capacity, down at the station. I'm sure your husband's attorney wouldn't want you disclosing anything that may incriminate him."

"Screw my soon-to-be-ex!" she spat. "I always suspected he was stepping out on me! You did me a favor by exposing him as the creep he is!" She shook her head mournfully. "That *poor, poor woman...* forgotten about in an unmarked grave all because that psychopath wanted to conceal his extramarital shenanigans."

"I'm sorry, Glori. Truly."

"Not as sorry as I am for marrying the cheating bastard." Glori fastened her cold fingers around my arm. "If it helps ease your worries any, sweetheart, I believe he never intended to do you any physical harm. He's truly a coward—always has been. I was the one in our marriage who had to dispose of insects and rodents." With a nasally laugh, she released me and wandered over to one of the stools at the kitchen island. She plopped down with the coordination of a rag doll. "While Ron was in jail, I packed his things. I came across something you might be able to use in your search for his missing mistress." Tongue darting out from her lips, she dug into the oversized designer purse hanging from her shoulder. "Just a minute...no, that's not it...I believe...ah! There's the buggar!"

Her fingers emerged with a postcard creased down the center. She held it up to show me the image of crystal clear waterfalls spilling into aqua blue water. "GREETINGS FROM CEBU ISLAND, PHILIPPINES" was printed on the top. After a moment, she thrusted the card at me. "Go ahead, read it."

I stepped forward and took the card, turning it around. It was addressed to Elizabeth Wells at an address in Destin, Florida.

Elizabeth Wells, as in Ginny's birth mother.

My dearest Elizabeth,

Each morning when I open my eyes, I miss seeing the beauty of your face beside me. I look forward to the day

when you can join me here in paradise. As hard as it is to
wait, I know your reunion with your daughter will be well
worth it.

Yours always, Alejandro xoxo

"A person has to ask themselves, how does Ron know Elizabeth and Alejandro?" Glori drawled. "We don't know anyone by those names. And how did that postcard end up in his possession?"

She was absolutely right. Who was Alejandro, and how did Ron end up with a postcard addressed to his lover's mother? When had this reunion between Ginny and Elizabeth taken place? Had Ron learned of Ginny's inheritance, and killed her so he could take it for himself?

I threw Glori a pasted-on smile. "Do you mind if I keep this?"

"Go ahead. It's as useless to me as my marriage to Ronald." Glori stood, swatting her hand through the air. "I hope it can help you right whatever wrongs he did to that poor dead woman."

"How did you get here?" I asked, watching her waddle back toward the door.

"I walked. It's not far."

"Hold on, I'm calling the Gorilla Bus."

I had to admit, the island no longer felt safe.

GRAYSON SPENT the majority of the flight to Destin on his phone in the back of the small jet, making arrangements using the private plane's Wifi network. I continually replayed the conversation with Glori in my head, trying to connect Ron to Ginny's mother in every way imaginable. *The most reasonable explanation,* I concluded, *involved Ginny somehow receiving the postcard and passing it along to Ron.* I was beginning to get the sickening feeling that Ron had in fact killed Ginny.

When the pilot announced it was time to prepare for landing, Grayson finished his final call and buckled into the seat across the tiny aisle from me. Seeing him in a light-colored sports jacket, shirt unbuttoned underneath, made it hard not to stare, and reminisce about the night I saw him shirtless as he rescued Lucky.

He plucked the postcard from my fingers. "You've been staring at this since we took off," he said, flipping it over several times. "This could be an important key to solving this case."

"Do you think it could somehow prove that Ron killed Ginny?"

He tilted his head. "I'm not sure. What's your gut telling you?"

"That I should've accepted the bag of peanuts they offered after takeoff." Remembering how Travis Parker died, I grimaced and straightened the skirt on my blue dress. "Speaking of peanuts, how do we know whether or not someone *intentionally* killed that private investigator?"

"We may never know." His fingers combed through his dark hair as he glanced out one of the oval windows. "I spoke with the detective on the case, and they weren't able to prove any foul play occurred. He didn't sound too interested in reopening the investigation."

"I can't shake the feeling that we're on the verge of discovering what happened to the woman Ron buried." As the plane began to descend, flipping my stomach, I clutched the armrests at my sides. I had never flown on anything smaller than a 737, and the private jet was hardly bigger than the tiki bar at Beach Bummers. "The facts keep circling back to Ginny and her family."

His gaze slipped over to me. "If you're right, this could all be over soon."

"When do we meet with Travis's colleague?"

"He said he'd be available as soon as we land."

The tug of excitement had me sitting a little taller. "Did he say whether or not he's willing to disclose everything in Travis's file?"

"One better—he's letting us hold onto the file for as long as we're in the area, and he offered to take us to Anton Wells's estate. You could be onto something when you suggested we interview the neighbors to see if they know anything about Anton's relationship with his daughter and Ginny." His warm hand covered mine. "I'll be glad once we've solved this, and you're able to sleep at night without letting Ginny's whereabouts eat at you."

"Like the visuals Ron described will be anything I'll forget about anytime soon." Although I supposed I would feel a little better knowing who had died that night. When the wheels connected with pavement, slightly jerking us forward, I slipped my hand out from beneath his.

The man hired to find Ginny was dead. What if it was because he had found the answers I was searching for when he paid a visit to the same destination in which Grayson and I were headed?

MELVIN "RISKY" Risk was a short, lithe man with an abundance of long black hair that hung like curtains around his narrow features and wrinkled brow. As he drove us through Destin, responding to each of Grayson's questions with stuttered breaths, his neck remained stiff. His clothes were wrinkled, and the odor of chewing tobacco clung to his pale skin.

Between questions, Grayson skimmed through Travis's file on the Wells family. "Did Travis say anything to you about Ginny or her grandfather before he died?"

"Only that he suspected he had found Ginny," Risky answered, his soprano pitch lowering. "Can't say I gave it too much thought until my receptionist brought it up. I'm starting to think she may be right. Anton Wells was worth a fortune."

Grayson's gaze caught mine. "He didn't mention to anyone *where* he thought she might be?"

"Nah, but I'd bet my life it had something to do with the grandfather's former residence. I don't know why else he would've been headed there the day he'd died. It had been years since the home was sold off by Anton's daughter."

"We were told by George Jones that Elizabeth Wells was last seen in the Philippine Islands." I slid forward on the backseat of Risky's older Tahoe, resting my hand on the back of the passenger's seat occupied by Grayson. "Did Travis mention whether or not she had gone there to meet someone? Perhaps someone named Alejandro?"

"You'd have to check the file," Risky told me. "Between arrangements for the funeral and all the calls from Travis's clients that I've been fielding, I haven't had a lot of time to dissect the details."

Risky turned off a heavily wooded highway and drove several blocks before white sand and palm trees came into view. Within minutes, we were surrounded by middle-class homes dotted along the gulf's shoreline. The homes quickly morphed into massive mansions that made our island's most exquisite homes resemble shacks. Behind elegant iron gates and grand entrances, some of the proper-ties stretched well beyond the length of an entire city block.

Outside of a four-level monstrosity that could've easily been mistaken for a luxury hotel, Risky parked at the curb.

"This is it?" I asked, eyeing the stone pillars and turrets beyond a reflecting pool in the center of the stone driveway.

"This was Anton's estate," Risky confirmed. He grabbed a soda can from the cupholder, spitting a gob of dark saliva inside. "Unless you need me, I'll wait out here."

"We're going to take our time canvassing the neighborhood," Grayson told him as he pulled on the passenger's door lever. "Go ahead and take off. I have your number in case I can think of any other questions for you." He motioned to the file tucked under his arm. "I'll bring this back to you in the morning."

"Good luck!" Risky called out as I exited the vehicle and walked around to join Grayson. A sense of doom washed over me as we watched Risky pull away.

Grayson nudged my side. "You all right?"

Although my stomach was in knots, I answered with a firm nod. I followed his lead through the property's open gate, making a note of the name engraved on a plaque secured to the iron gate. "Anita Wellington."

"Anita must be one wealthy woman," Grayson commented.

We continued to hike across the long stone driveway, veering around the reflection pool in which a set of swans bathed themselves. "Rich people spend their money on the weirdest things," I muttered while gaping at the beautiful creatures.

Grayson didn't hesitate in climbing the grand steps leading up to a set of double doors. He didn't have a chance to knock before they swung open. My gaze swept over a woman's large chest spilling out from a tiny pink bikini, and connected with a set of mismatched eyes.

"Ginny," I gasped.

SEVENTEEN

"*Ginny?*" the beautiful brunette repeated with quick, high-pitched laughter. Her slender legs shifted several times. "Honey, I'm afraid you have the wrong address. There isn't anyone named *Ginny* at this residence."

I tilted my head. What were the chances a different woman had the same unusual eyes as Ginny and the late, great Bowie? "But your—"

She interrupted with a curt, "Nope. Sorry."

She *had to* be lying. "What about—" I protested.

"Nuh-uh." she snapped. "Still not her." She offered Grayson a hand dripping in brilliant gemstones. "The name's Anita Wellington. I'd love to make *your* acquaintance, you gorgeous man."

"Detective Grayson Rivers," he answered in a formal tone, giving her hand a quick shake.

The woman's thick eyelashes fluttered against her sharp cheekbones. "I assure you I'm a law-abiding citizen," she teased with a short, jerky shake of her head. "What on earth could a *detective* want with little ol' me?"

"I'm hoping you might be able to answer some questions we have about this property's previous owner, Anton Wells."

The woman's blood-red fingernails fanned over her chest. She feigned a cartoonish expression worthy of the actresses on one of Teenie's soap operas. "I'm afraid I never knew Mr. Wells, god rest his soul. The only contacts I had when purchasing this property involved his estate's attorney and the realtor."

Judging by her smooth, youthful skin, she was around Ginny's age—despite the effort to make herself sound like a senior citizen. She may not have been blonde the way everyone remembered, but a change of hair color was the easiest disguise for someone who didn't want to be found.

Fingers coiled around Grayson's tattooed arm, I tugged until he bent to my level. "Remember how Sasha said Ginny had mismatched eyes, like David

Bowie's?" I frantically whispered. "And this woman has a...uh...you know..."

When he titled his head in question, I made an exaggerated motion toward my chest.

"Right," he whispered back. "I was thinking the same thing. Follow my lead." He swung his gaze back to the woman. "You're saying you never met Mr. Wells's daughter, Elizabeth, or his granddaughter, Ginny? I believe his granddaughter would've been in control of the estate at the time of the sale."

The woman's mismatched eyes flickered upward as she slipped a hand inside her long, dark locks to scratch her scalp. "I did notice a stunning young woman waiting in the attorney's office at the time of the sale. I didn't catch her name, though." She gave an aggressive shake of her head, ruffling her dark hair. "I'm sorry I couldn't help you and your cute little friend, detective. If you'll excuse me, the sunshine's calling my name." Stepping back, she began to close the doors in our faces. "Have a wonderful day!"

Grayson's foot shot out, prying the doors back open. "Not so fast." He plucked the postcard from his jacket, and held it up between them. "Maybe there's something you can tell me about this."

Every ounce of color swept from the woman's

face. "W-where did you get that?" she whispered. With a trembling hand, she reached for it.

"Why don't you tell us, *Ms. Wellington,*" he replied, allowing her to take the postcard. "Or should I say, *Ms. Jones?*"

Her shoulders rounded, erasing her perfect posture. "I hoped this gig would last a little longer before I was forced to take on another persona," she responded in a dull tone. "I mean, look at this place. Who in their right mind would want to leave?" She snarled in my direction. "Who are *you*, and how in the hell did you know it was me?"

Grayson cut in before I had a chance to answer. "There's a warrant out for your arrest, Miss Jones. Unless you have a good explanation behind the death of the woman Ron Finkle buried on your behalf, I'm afraid I have to take you in."

With sweeping arm gestures, she nudged the doors open wide. "You may as well make yourselves comfortable."

THE PROPERTY'S backyard put every resort I'd ever set foot on to shame. Among a meticulously groomed collection of swaying palm trees and white quartz sand, a massive infinity pool and nearly equally sized hot tub overlooked the sparkling blue Gulf of Mexico. Dozens of white hammocks hung beneath endless bulb lights and lanterns. Contemporary teak furniture with white cushions surrounded the pool, many arranged beneath white cabanas stocked with bars and flat screen televisions.

Wrapped like a burrito inside a white terrycloth robe, Ginny let out a long, low sigh as she plopped onto a couch across from us. "What happened that night was an accident. You can ask Ron. He saw everything."

"Who was she?" I blurted from Grayson's side, vibrating from head to toe. "It was your birth mom, wasn't it?" I was well-aware I shouldn't insert myself into an official interrogation, but the intensity was enough to make my heart burst. "How'd she die?"

Ginny tipped her head back and released a youthful giggle. "Aren't you an eager little thing? Hoping to get an 'A' on your homework assignment?"

"Why don't you start from the beginning?" Grayson suggested, stilling my bouncing knee with one hand. "When did your grandfather pass away? When did you last work at Beach Bummers?"

A fair-haired muscular man with a neatly

groomed beard entered our circle of furniture, presenting Ginny with a cocktail glass. A blue cocktail parasol embellished the orange liquid. The man only wore a black satin Speedo, and a matching bowtie. My jaw may have dropped a little when I caught sight of his tanned, tight buns.

"Your afternoon drink, beautiful," he told Ginny in a thick Australian accent. "Would you like me to fetch two more for your mates?"

"None for us," Grayson answered, lifting a hand.

"That won't be necessary, Liam." Ginny took the glass and watched with delight as the man bent down. His lips brushed over each of her cheeks. "Thank you, my love," she told him.

"My pleasure," he chirped. Before strutting away, he tossed a flirty wink in my direction.

The question heavy on my mind tumbled from my lips before I could sensor myself. "Do you make everyone on your staff dress like Chippendales dancers?"

Grayson's grip tightened on my knee.

"Liam's my live-in lover," she answered with a coy smile. "Well...*one* of them, anyway." Her mismatched eyes traveled down to where Grayson's fingers made an indentation in my skin. "Are you going to sit there and tell me this beautiful man of yours doesn't dress for you in a way that's pleasing to *your* eyes?"

Grayson coughed and recoiled his hand with the speed of someone who had been physically burned.

"He's not 'mine'," I blurted, frustrated with the warm glow of an oncoming blush that filled my cheeks.

Ginny's smile grew as she arched back, tapping her long nails against the back of the couch. I didn't like the way she eyeballed Grayson with a new appreciation. "What a shame."

"How about that timeline, Miss Jones?" he prodded, retrieving a small notepad from inside his sports coat.

"Oh yes." Her smile slipped. "I believe my grandfather died around a month before I last worked for Smith." She paused to take a sip of her drink with a faraway look. "I think it's been around five and a half years since I left the island."

Grayson scribbled something down. "*Why* did you leave the island?"

One of her hands rolled through the air. "I had no other choice. I was afraid no one would believe I *hadn't* committed murder."

"Why wouldn't they believe you?" Grayson asked.

I scooted forward on the couch, sensing all of my questions were about to be answered.

"Because it was no secret to anyone that she hated me!" Ginny snapped. Her symmetrical features creased with a deep frown. "Everyone knew she had contested my grandfather's will! How would it look if the police had learned she'd died after she'd come down to the island, demanding I give her every last cent he'd left to me!"

The truth clicked into place. "It *was* Elizabeth Wells," I confirmed, touching my stomach. "And Ron hid her body."

"*That* wasn't *my idea!*" She bolted to her feet, spilling half of her drink down the front of her robe. "But what else could I do? That woman was a raving lunatic! She couldn't accept the fact that her father loved his abandoned granddaughter more than his spoiled brat of a daughter! It was her own damn fault when she tripped and fell! If she hadn't, she likely would've given herself a heart attack with all that jealous rage!"

"You're saying you never laid a hand on her?" Grayson confirmed.

"No!" Tears leaked down Ginny's cheeks as she repeatedly shook her head. "I didn't touch her even though she kept pushing me over and over! She promised her lover that they'd build a castle on some tropical island, and she refused to leave until I handed over the money so she could fulfill her promise!"

With a gentle look, Grayson held one hand up. "Take a breath, Miss Jones. I can understand this must be upsetting. Why don't you walk me through everything you did after you realized Elizabeth was dead?"

She heaved a stuttering sigh and wiped the tears from her face. Her knees wobbled as she slowly lowered back down to the couch. "I had never met my real mom until that night. I was so excited when I first laid eyes on her. How could I not be? We looked so much alike—she was gorgeous. Then she started *yelling*. And let me tell you, that woman could *yell*. I dodged a bullet when she gave me away. Groundings by her would've been nothing less than pure torture." Her knuckles dabbed the corners of her eyes. "I was so relieved to see Ron until he caught her by surprise. Let me tell you, when she fell, her face flattened like a pancake. I'd never seen anything so horrifying." Grimacing, she paused to throw back the rest of her drink. "Once I realized she wasn't getting back up, I started to call nine-one-one. Ron stopped me, said they'd never believe it was an accident. I must've gone into shock at that point. I merely watched helplessly while he checked her pockets for anything that would reveal her identity. All he came up with was that postcard and a key to the car she'd driven down to the island. That's when he told me to leave the island, and never come back."

Grayson frantically scribbled without glancing away from the notebook. "What'd he do with the body?"

"I didn't ask because I didn't want to know. I never spoke to Ron again. A few months later, my grandfather's attorney got a call from the Destin airport saying Elizabeth's car needed to be removed from long term parking. There must've been a mixup on the flight because they claimed her name showed up on the manifesto."

Grayson's eyes met hers. "Did your grandfather's attorney help you become Anita Wellington?"

"I'm going to assume that's a rhetorical question." Her breath caught with a forced laugh. "I'm an extremely wealthy woman, Detective. I can buy whatever my heart desires. My grandfather didn't want my mother to know we spent time together, so *no one* in his world really knew me. I was essentially hiding in plain sight." Her thick, butterfly-like lashes fluttered as a sassy grin puckered her lips. "I could arrange for anything to become a reality. If *you* ever had an inkling to run away and start a new life, I could make that happen with the snap of my fingers."

"Is that an attempt at a bribe?" Grayson asked, molars clenched.

"Of course not!" Still grinning, she narrowed her eyes. "I'm just saying a woman on the run can get lonely at times. Besides, I didn't kill Elizabeth. I have nothing to hide now that the truth is out in the open." She dug her fingers inside the empty cocktail glass and fished out a macadamia nut. "Seriously, Liam!" Clicking her tongue, she chucked it into a floral bush. "He *knows* I despise these things!"

Grayson's gaze surveyed the bush. "What was that?"

"A macadamia nut." Appearing agitated, she shrugged. "So what?"

With a rush of adrenaline, I straightened my spine. "Wait! Are you drinking a Nutty Ocho Rios?"

Ginny's eyes lit with amusement. "After you graduate high school, you'd make an excellent cocktail waitress."

I pivoted around to face Grayson. "They're made with macadamia nut liqueur."

Grayson's brow lifted in Ginny's direction. "Does Liam offer that same drink to all your guests?"

"Duh—they're my favorite!" She titled her head. "Want one?"

"Have you ever met Travis Parker with Parker Investigations?" he asked.

"Why yes." She lifted her hands before lacing them together. "Matter of fact, he was just here the other day."

Grayson motioned to her glass. "Did he drink one of those?"

"Not while he was here, but he took one for the road."

I exchanged a wide-eyed look with Grayson. Ginny may have been guilty of *other* things, including keeping her birth mother's accidental death a secret, but it seemed she hadn't intentionally murdered anyone. The knot in my chest loosened.

Ginny's svelte lips gaped. "Hold on. Is that how you found me? Did that sleaze-ball go against our agreement to keep my identity on the down-low? I paid him rather handsomely to keep his mouth shut!"

"Mr. Parker is unable to break your agreement," Grayson assured her with a firm shake of his head. "He died from a nut allergy."

Her hand flew to her open mouth. "Oh my god! And you think—" Lips screwed together, she wove both of her arms around her waist. "You know what? I'm not saying another word until I speak with my attorney."

"Suit yourself." Grayson stood, rubbing a hand over the back of his neck. "Regardless, you'll need to come along with me to the local police station. If everything you said is true, you shouldn't have too much to worry about aside from a few misdemeanors. Someone with your clean record will most likely get off pretty easily." He retrieved his phone from inside his sports coat. "Stay put while I make the arrangements."

"Well this sucks." Slouching deeper into the couch, Ginny's eyes honed in on me the moment he walked away. "What are you? The next generation of *Jump Street*?"

Hands lifted at my sides, I stood. "Actually, I'm just a cocktail waitress from Beach Bummers. Smith hired me a few years after you disappeared."

Her heavily bronzed cheeks rounded with a wide smile. "How is that old stud muffin? Does anyone else I would know still work there?"

"Smith's his same old ornery self. And both Finn and Sasha are still around. I'm sure they'd send their regards." My eyes flickered down to her chest peeking out of her robe. "They definitely remembered...ah...you."

"Finn?" she squealed, clapping with the energy of a baby seal. "Oh my god! How is that beautiful man? Is he still single?"

"I doubt he's changed any since you've seen him."

"You'll have to tell him hello from me! Or maybe I should come see him." She nibbled on a perfect fingernail. "What do you think? Do you think he'd want another hookup?"

"I think you'll have a chance to see him in person *real* soon."

I caught Grayson watching us, a corner of his mouth quirked in amusement. Ducking my head, I doubted I should've been carrying on any kind of lighthearted conversation with his detainee.

Ginny let out a dreamy sigh. "If you're not really with that yummy detective, do you mind if I make my move?"

I told myself it wouldn't be polite to laugh. *It must've taken some nerve to be in her position and assume something so bold.* Lifting my eyebrows, I turned to her. "Liam wouldn't mind?"

"His work visa expires soon, and I'll be back on

my own." One of her shoulders lifted to her chin. "I wasn't kidding about being lonely."

"In that case, go for it."

I bit back the start of a smile as I turned away from her and started for Grayson. I wanted to put as much distance between myself and Ginny as possible.

Grayson muttered something into his phone before slipping it back into his pocket and meeting my gaze. "The local PD will be here soon to bring her in. I'll ride along with them, and a uniformed officer will take you to the hotel."

My lungs heaved with a calming breath. "It's finally over."

He looped an arm around my back and gave a gentle squeeze. "You did good, kiddo."

EIGHTEEN

I'd witnessed hundreds of Florida sunsets, but when the sky exploded behind the Destin hotel in a stunning array of pastels, I was filled with a sense of tranquility unlike any before. Exhaustion loosened my muscles as I watched young families splash around in the shallow end of the flamingo-shaped pool. When was the last time I'd allowed myself to truly relax? My life had become crazy in the search for Ginny. If Chief Shaw asked me to stay on at the station, I'd be forced to sit down with Smith for a heart-to-heart. While I wasn't anywhere near ready to quit Beach Bummers, it wouldn't be long before I'd be drained from working two full-time jobs.

Once a chill bit through the evening air, I threw

on my oversized Beyoncé t-shirt from her last tour, and headed to the hotel's tiki bar. Nothing about it was as grand or as welcoming as Beach Bummers, and their burgers were lacking without Smith's secret seasoning, but the bartenders and patrons were just as friendly, and the drinks were decent. Grayson reported in with several texts throughout the night to let me know they'd processed Ginny, and he likely wouldn't arrive at the hotel until after midnight.

Two and a half fuzzy navels later, I headed up to my room paid for by my new employer's expense credit card. With the remainder of my last cocktail on the nightstand at my side, I scoured social media for Elizabeth Wells in Destin. For whatever reason, it felt like the respectful thing to do. I had seen her in death, and wanted to witness her living her best life.

I quickly stumbled across a handful of pictures involving a blonde woman that had been made public, one involving Anton Wells's unmistakable backyard. Ginny resembled her birth mother in many ways, sharing the same long legs, sharp cheekbones, and augmented chest. Elizabeth's long, silky locks were a shade of honey that perfectly suited her fair complexion, and her eyes were the same brilliant blue as one of Ginny's. She appeared youthful enough in the last post that she could've passed as Ginny's sister.

In most of the pictures, Elizabeth's lips were pressed together in what Molly would refer to as a "constipated smile." Nearly every shot was taken somewhere tropical with blue skies and crystal waters in the background. In a few she wore colorful dresses, and in others she wore provocative swimsuits. There were always sunglasses perched on her head, although never the same pair. Had she shown a natural smile, she could've been a successful influencer on social media. For all I knew about her, maybe she was.

The very last image, a selfie, involved Elizabeth cocooned in the arms of a handsome, dark skinned man. They posed in front of the same set of Philippine waterfalls pictured on the postcard Glori had found among Ron's belongings.

I swiped my fingers over the mouse pad, letting the pointer hover over the picture. Another profile had been tagged.

"Alejandro dela Cruz," I read.

Elizabeth beamed with a dazzling smile in the picture, flashing her teeth on full display. With tears stinging my eyes, I zoomed in on the image and moved it around until I spotted the corner of a gold tooth among her pearly whites.

Rather than feeling exhausted, a fulfilling tired-ness seeped into my bones. Elizabeth and Alejandro looked happy. It was the visual I wanted to forever associate with the woman I'd helped. With the truth brought to light, Alejandro would be able to properly mourn the loss of his "dearest Elizabeth," and move on.

For the first time in over a week, I slept like the dead.

———

ONCE WE BOARDED the private jet bound for Tampa the following morning, Grayson slept as hard as I had the night before. I logged into the plane's wifi to let Molly know Ginny was alive and well. She tried to pressure me into revealing the identity of the woman they'd found on the island, but I was careful not to say anything. As we had checked out of the hotel and waited for our transportation to the airport, Grayson told me Elizabeth's death would be plastered across national news once the reporters in Destin caught word of Ginny's arrest.

Grayson remained relatively quiet after we landed, and didn't have much to say as he steered his Bronco toward the highway that would take us home. I tilted my head toward the warm sun and took in lungfuls at a time of the fresh air. As we neared the island, the atmosphere somehow felt different, as if my body had become attuned to my new home.

After we crossed the first of many bridges in the final stretch, Grayson cleared his throat. "A judge in Destin released Ginny on the conditions that she relinquish her passports—both real and forged, and that she wear an ankle bracelet until her first hearing. The island's prosecutor filed a request with a local judge for her to appear in our county court as soon as they're able to transport her down. Unless her attorney and the prosecutor come up with an agreement, it could be a long, drawn-out process. I doubt the matter will go to trial, but I've been caught by surprise with other cases in the past."

"Do you still believe she won't go to jail?" I asked, wrangling my wind-whipped locks into a knot on top of my head.

"From what I understand, the prosecutor plans to hold off on any kind of sentencing until the forensic pathologists submit their final report on Elizabeth's remains. If her death is ruled an accident, Ginny will most likely be sentenced to fines and some community service as punishment for not properly reporting her mother's death."

"Do you think she was truthful about what happened with her mom and Travis Parker?"

He nodded thoughtfully. "Once she met with her attorney, she told the local detectives nearly the same story about Elizabeth's death being accidental. And she asserts she had no knowledge of Travis's allergy. The Destin police will re-investigate the circumstances surrounding his death before they rule whether or not her involvement was unintentional."

"How do you know whether or not she was throwing Ron under the bus when she claimed it was all his idea to conceal Elizabeth's death?"

"She broke down in tears a few times, admitting she was in love with Ron, and would've done anything he suggested. I've worked with her type countless times. She's not exactly weak, but she's easily manipulated by others."

"Does that mean Ron will be in more serious trouble?"

"That's up to the prosecutor to decide." Behind his sunglasses, he threw me a sideways glance. "Did you really tell Ginny it was okay to make a move on me?"

"She wanted to know whether or not I cared if she asked you out." Heat rushed to my face when I lifted both shoulders. "I said no."

He returned his gaze to the road, nodding thoughtfully. "So you won't mind if I take her out once they remove her ankle bracelet?"

My lips desperately tried to form a response. *Grayson had agreed to a date with her?*

Then his serious demeanor cracked, and he let out a hearty chuckle. "Relax, Zoey. I just wanted to see you squirm the same way I squirmed when she asked me if I wanted to grab dinner sometime." Amusement lingered in his grin. "Seriously, though. Why would you tell her that?"

"Because I knew you'd turn her down."

The corners of his mouth twitched. "What made you so sure?"

"I know you pretty well by now." Turning away from him, I tapped my fingers on the side of his truck along to the Alice in Chains tune thumping from his speakers. "She's not your type."

"Really?" he asked, his voice light with sarcasm. "Then who is?"

"You seem to like cute, smart little monkeys who enjoy solving mysteries."

He let out a deep, rolling laugh that vibrated in

my belly. *"Cute little monkeys*? Honestly, Zo. Where do you come up with this stuff?"

I turned to him with a pointed stare. "You forgot 'smart'."

"Okay, fine. You have me pegged." He lifted one hand in a gesture of surrender. "But if I'm going to take you out on that date like I promised, we have to agree on a few things."

My entire body thrummed. "Like what?"

"As long as you continue to work at the station, we have to keep it professional whenever either one of us is on the clock. I don't want the chief to know we're seeing each other—at least not for now."

"Agreed." I nodded eagerly. "I promise I'll control myself."

"Most importantly, we can't rush this thing. Even if we make the mutual decision to become inclusive, I'm not ready to make any big commitments. I moved too quickly with Bexley, and her rejection left a pretty big scar." Eyes dancing with mischief, he glanced over at me. "Besides, we wouldn't want to give Lucky any mixed signals about his *daddy and mommy* getting together."

"His best interests come first," I agreed with another teasing nod.

"And now that you have this bug to 'solve

mysteries' as you said, you have to promise you won't lie or hide anything significant from me regarding a case *or your safety*." His stern gaze held mine. "That condition is a deal breaker."

"I could keep telling you I'm sorry until I'm blue in the face, but I'm starting to understand it's going to take a significant gesture on my part for you to trust me again." Turning sideways in my seat, I set my hand on the seat behind him. "I won't let you down."

"Oh, and one more thing." He caught a wayward red strand of hair in his fingers, giving it a light tug. "Stop referring to yourself as 'cute'. The smart, playful woman with a big heart that I look forward to spending more time with is clearly beautiful." He threw me a gorgeous smile that made my heart screech to a halt. "It's an injustice to call the Zoey Zastrow I know anything less."

QUINN'S BLUEBERRY MOSCOW MULE

- Muddled blueberries (I smash a few in the bottom of the cup with the mint leaves, and save some for embellishments.)
- 1 or 2 mint leaves (super optional...I never have any on hand.)
- Ginger beer (I like to use diet so I can tell myself at least I'm "drinking healthy. " Also, you can substitute ginger ale with

ginger beer, but the flavor won't be as strong.)

- A splash of juice from a lime (save a wedge for the rim of the mug.)
- Blueberry vodka (Western Son is my favorite! Depending on your level of party mode, use one or two shots, and fill the rest with ginger beer.)

Directions: Mix ingredients together in a copper mug or any other kind of glass. Drinking from a copper mug is awesome as they keep your mule ice cold, but they aren't 100% necessary. Full disclaimer, I've read long-term use of copper can cause health problems, but not all copper mugs have the potential to be poisonous.

Kick back and enjoy with a friend or your favorite female sleuth!

Be the first to know when Quinn's next
book is available! Subscribe to Quinn's newsletter:
www.quinnavery.com/subscribe

FOLLOW QUINN
Bookbub:
www.bookbub.com/profile/quinn-avery
Amazon: bit.ly/QAamazon
Goodreads: www.goodreads.com/QuinnAvery

QUINN AVERY is a bestselling author (under
various pen names) of over 30 romantic suspense,
young adult paranormal, and mystery novels. When
not involved in the madness of their 4 children's
lives, Quinn and her husband divide their time
between rural Minnesota and Lake Shetek, MN.

www.QuinnAvery.com
quinn@quinnavery.com

ACKNOWLEDGMENTS

Special thanks to Najla Qamber for coming up with the coolest cover ever! I adore working with you, and love how you were able to give me exactly what I had envisioned!

Thank you to Lisa Frommie and Rena Zierke for your constant willingness to answer my odd technical questions!

Big thanks to Corrie Hanson and Christy Freeberg for your willingness to be my constant lab rats!

Thanks to Jodi Henley for your expertise!

And finally, biggest of thank yous of all to my husband, kids, other family and friends for always supporting my career!

Made in the USA
Monee, IL
04 May 2023

33029329R00142